THE AFTERLIFE JOURNEY

THE FIRST 300 YEARS

by Glenn Bennetts

Publisher: Inspiring Publishers

PO. Box 159 Calwell ACT Australia 2905 Email: publishaspg@gmail.com
http://www.inspiringpublishers.com

National Library of Australia Cataloguing-in-Publication entry

Author: Bennetts, Glenn Earle

Title: The afterlife journey/Glenn Earle Bennetts.

ISBN: 9780987346360 (pbk.)

Subjects: Future life–Fiction.

Dewey Number: A823.4

PROLOGUE

A picture flashed into my mind and I willed myself towards it with every ounce of my being. Instantly, I was transported to the spot, a large, rotating hole in the fabric of space. To me, it looked like a huge funnel lying on its side. The exterior of the orifice was a yellowish white while the interior, or what I could see of it, was a foreboding black. It was hard to see inside because of the pale, newborn Auras streaming from its innermost parts like a beautiful cascading fireworks display; a kaleidoscope of colours all flowing in one direction. In morbid fascination I watched, aghast at the never-ending volume of dead and wondered if any of my dear ones were amongst this vast multitude.

I sensed no thought or feeling from any of them. Trance-like, they streamed ever closer to Nyame and the first transition, blindly being pulled like iron shavings to a magnet.

"At least these are the lucky ones who will have a chance," I comforted myself, overwhelmed at witnessing the tangible evidence of what had been happening on the Earth. I could have wept at such a terrible loss of life and the suffering these people had undergone before death had claimed them.

I glanced at Niara and was shocked beyond belief.

"Niara, you have a form!"

I could see the ghostly outline of a female body.

"Yes, our aural energy leaves a faint imprint of the body we leave behind on Earth. It stays with us forever."

"Why couldn't I see it before now and why don't I have one?"

"The reason why you could not see my image before is because the void is too dark to see such a faint outline and as to your second question, you do have an imprint. You just need to look harder."

I imagined putting my hand out in front of me and sure enough, the faint outline of my hand appeared.

"Wow! That's awesome."

After a quick investigation, I decided I was far more interested in looking at Niara's shape than my own.

I could now see that the two twinkling stars formed part of her eyes and the colourful band above them could almost be mistaken for hair. Her nose was broader than most Caucasians but in perfect proportion to her face. She had high cheekbones and her lips were beautiful and full. Her neck was long and slender atop what appeared to be a lithe, athletic body. There was something special about her which I couldn't quite put my finger on, almost as if she was royalty.

"She would have been stunning to look at in the flesh," I thought as Niara broke the spell.

"We must hurry Grant. We may move through the wormhole freely here. Follow me."

Once inside, I saw hundreds of Guides heading against the continuous flow of former humanity. The Guides looked like an army of ghosts disappearing into a black cavern. Joining them, we floated along the ever-narrowing corridor of space. Up ahead, every few seconds I could see a flash of blinding light followed by a sizzling, cracking sound.

"What's happening Niara?" I whispered, trying to keep the trepidation out of my voice.

"That is the narrowest point ahead, Grant. You must be exceedingly careful not to be drawn in. This is where the energies are being compressed and suffering destruction," she replied tensely.

Drawing ever closer, the problem became clearly evident. The Auras were truly packed in like sardines. It was as if there was a terrible traffic pile-up with horrendous results. Even as we watched, we could see the build-up of heat and energy. It felt as if we were waiting for a volcano to erupt.

Suddenly, there was a mind-numbing explosion and the energies at the centre were obliterated, freeing the wormhole for a matter of seconds, allowing thousands of Auras through until the incoming tide jammed new ones tight again. It was sickening and absolutely fear-inspiring. It didn't take long before the whole process repeated itself and it appeared that the ones getting through were equalled by the ones being destroyed.

"Watch as the Guides time their run Grant. They must get through and past the incoming Auras before the passage blocks again. There is no escape. If they are caught, they will perish. Once they get through, they will make their way to the end of the worm hole and then project themselves to Earth."

"Why can't they just project themselves to Earth from here?"

"There is no projection through the wormhole. It is the control station in and out of the transitions. It is a safeguard against any unforeseen surprises," explained Niara.

Fleetingly, I thought to question her further but decided against it. I needed to focus on the task ahead. Steeling myself, I watched as the Guides, ten at a time, lined up, waited for the ordeal of the explosion and then quickly floated through the ensuing gap. Two groups made the difficult navigation. Soon it would be our turn. I watched and tried to prepare myself for the timing of my run.

Everything seemed to be progressing smoothly until the sixth group made their attempt. As they were making their way through, one Guide appeared to be knocked off balance by a cluster of Auras coming from the opposite direction. He, in turn, was pushed into another Guide. The mishap only cost both of them one or two seconds but it was enough. Before they could progress any further, they were surrounded and completely engulfed by the Auras. They were hopelessly snared.

I mentally reached out to connect with them, anguish ripping and tearing at me, only to find myself being drawn into the death trap.

"Let go or you will also perish!" Niara demanded hoarsely.

As painful as it was, my reaction was instant and I released contact, springing back to Niara's side. Almost all colour seemed to have drained from her. The colour of her aura was virtually white and I felt her pain wounding me.

"You cannot help them Grant. This is the sacrifice they were prepared to make and they are doing it with peace in their minds. This may also be our fate. I have lived many thousands of years in the Afterlife and I am prepared to forego my place in the scheme of Nyame, but you Grant, need not do this. There is no shame if you should change your mind and return to your transition," she offered me gently.

"I will not leave," I managed to choke out before the explosion occurred which wiped out the Guides.

DEDICATION

THIS BOOK IS DEDICATED TO MY MOTHER
MAJ-LIS BENNETTS.

THROUGHOUT LIFE [AND PERHAPS EVEN AFTER] WE ALL
NEED GUIDES AND MENTORS. ONE OF THOSE CRUCIAL
PERIODS IS FROM ZERO TO SEVEN YEARS OLD, THE
BUILDING BLOCKS OF LIFE'S JOURNEY. FROM A STRUGGLING
DYSFUNCTIONAL FAMILY MY MOTHER ALWAYS FOUND
TIME FOR HER CHILDREN AND MADE EACH ONE OF US
FEEL SPECIAL AND LOVED.
THE MOST IMPORTANT JOB A MOTHER CAN EVER HAVE.

FOREWORD

Grant Sanders is your pretty average Australian bricklayer but with an incredible thirst for knowledge. An atheist, he doesn't believe in all that religion expounds about heaven and hell, or at least he didn't until his unexpected death. From that moment on, Grant found he had a lot to learn. The lessons and experiences he'd gone through in his former existence were nothing compared to what he would now discover.

He thought he had it all worked out, but eventually discovers many things come back to haunt him. His relationship with his father, his problem solving strategies and a secret that he believed he'd buried a long time ago. He discovered that death was definitely not easy!

With the help of those in the Afterlife, Grant begins an amazing journey that is to take him through a minefield of obstacles and complications. Even his former loved ones are involved with a life and death battle on Earth. Could Grant help? Would life be changed? These are the questions that may make all the difference.

Through it all Grant is sustained by memories of his wife Laura, and their family. Does love find a way? Only time will tell.

Grant's story is a tale of adventure, learning and turmoil spanning thousands of years and crossing the continents. It is a story to challenge the mind, indulge the senses and rollercoaster the emotion. This book was sixteen years in the making, fifteen of those years inside the author's head.

Now, at last, it is confined to the pages of this book. May you as the reader enjoy your time and travel with Grant in the Afterlife Journey.

I would sincerely like to thank my sister Serena, for the enormous amount of help she gave me; and to my daughter Calyce, for her invaluable input into the structure of the book. I would also like to thank my wife, Debbie, and brother, Laurie, for all their helpful advice.

It is with sincere appreciation that I would like to acknowledge Anna Dytlewski and Peter Owen for all their help with editing this manuscript for publication. Finally, thank you to my other two children, Leif and Teale, for their support and enthusiasm.

ABOUT THE AUTHOR

Glenn Bennetts lives in Queensland, Australia and has been a bricklayer for over thirty-seven years.

As a teenager, Glenn was heavily involved with horses, and in that time period, had over one hundred and twenty pets in a small backyard in suburbia. He bought his first house when he was twenty.

He met his wife, Debbie, in Mount Isa while traveling around Australia. Happily married for twenty-five years, they have three children.

Debbie and Glenn spent a number of years traveling around Australia and New Zealand before heading over to Europe and the U.S.A.

Glenn has been interested in astronomy, cosmology, evolution, philosophy and religious philosophy for all of his adult life. He has also been an avid golfer for the last thirty years.

The mechanical and repetitious lifestyle of a bricklayer left Glenn with endless hours to speculate and philosophise on questions such as; what could an Afterlife be like? What would its purpose be if you didn't take a strictly religious view? How could you try to fit it in with a more scientific view? Those questions and many more inspired the writing of this book series.

CHAPTER I

hoosh. The six iron sliced through the air and I watched as the ball arced smoothly into the clear blue sky, sailed gracefully to the green, and landed with a soft double plop.

"Top shot mate," my friend Noel congratulated me.

"You better watch out; I'm in top form today."

"I reckon that was just a fluke," my other friend Dave ribbed me. "I haven't given up on winning that sandwich yet."

"We'll see mate, we'll see."

People would always laugh about our strange bets.

"A sandwich, you're really playing for a sandwich?" they would ask.

"Yep, we sure do."

We have been playing for sandwiches for years. Whoever lost the previous week had to shout when the golf cart came around with the food and drinks. Other golfers couldn't understand why we didn't play for money but none of us were really gamblers, particularly me.

15

I recalled a time about fifteen years ago, when I'd thought up a system for roulette while at work. I told my brother Richard, who was living here in Queensland at the time, and a Kiwi bricklayer named Lance, who I employed, about the system. They were both keen to give it a go, so off we went to the casino. The first time we won $1,500 in two hours and they were ecstatic. I, on the other hand, hated every second of it.

Don't get me wrong. Winning the money was great but the stress of sometimes having hundreds of dollars riding on the spin of a wheel was nerve-wracking and when the wrong colour came up, excruciatingly painful.

We ended up going to the casino half a dozen times over the next twelve months and only lost once; the second time we went. We had won $2,000 after two hours and I wanted to stop. The other two desperately wanted to keep playing for another thirty minutes, so reluctantly, I sat back and watched.

It wasn't long before I noticed Richard had stopped following the system. I walked over and asked, "What are you up to?"

"I'm feeling lucky," he replied.

In twenty minutes Richard and Lance had lost the $2,000 we had won, plus a further $500. A valuable lesson I suppose and from then on, there were never any arguments about the system, or when to leave. When Richard returned to Canberra and Lance to New Zealand, I was so relieved about not having to face the stress of gambling that I never went back.

"Grant, are you going to have a putt or look at the scenery all day?" quipped Dave.

Laughing, we ambled over to our respective golf balls.

"This is the life. No wonder I love playing this game," I reflected as the ball shaved the edge of the hole, finishing a few inches past.

I really enjoyed the camaraderie, the exercise, the competition and the sheer beauty. The sun shone, birds whistled and chirped in the gently swaying trees and dew sparkled on the verdant grass like chips of crystal. I loved to watch the bearded dragon lizards bask in the sun. If you moved slowly enough, you could walk right up to them and stroke them under the chin. I breathed the fresh, sweet air deeply and exhaled, feeling my body relax as I tapped in for a par.

My wife Laura was getting a bit weary of me taking off two or three days a week to hit the ball around but hey, isn't that what retirement is all about? I'd worked hard for more than forty years doing my job as a bricklaying contractor and I had the knees and back to prove it. I reckoned I deserved a bit more 'me' time, especially since the kids had grown up and moved away.

"All work and no play makes Grant a dull boy," I laughed, remembering the old saying as I teed up and then drove the ball straight down the middle of the fairway.

"It's good for me," I'd tell Laura. "You're the one telling me I'm putting on too much weight."

Mind you, the chips and beers we scoffed after each game probably weren't helping much, but you only live once, right? My mates would have given me a hard time if I'd told them I was trying to watch my waistline, although I had to admit we weren't really getting a great deal of exercise. If we walked, it was at a stroll, or we'd often take a golf cart. It was faster and easier that way.

"Nice drive Grant. Anywhere in that area would suit me nicely," said Dave as he practised his swing and then hit it within ten feet of my own.

"Great shot!" Noel and I echoed as we ambled down the manicured fairway.

Anyway, Laura was easy going and I didn't think she minded too much. Probably glad to have me out of her hair, if truth be told. All our married life she'd kept herself busy, working to begin with and then staying at home to take care of our three children as they came along. We agreed that her staying home was more important than the additional income.

She always seemed to have some project on the go, whether it was housework, caring for injured wild animals, involving herself with the kids' activities or helping out at the local school. She was a keen photographer as well as an avid birdwatcher. She could rattle off a bird's name and take a photo of it quicker than I could say, "What bird?" I used to tease her about being a workaholic, particularly when she got upset with me for sitting around the house too long.

We've had some great adventures though; skydiving, bungy jumping, mountain climbing and swimming with crocodiles when our boat sank. You name it, we've done it. I think that, and good communication, was the reason why our marriage is still going strong. We always have plenty to talk about. On top of everything else, she's been a great help to me with the bookwork for the business, doing the banking and taking phone calls. All the time consuming stuff I hated doing. I'm more a doer than a talker.

"I made my money by working hard and fast, not talking about it," I thought as I reached into my bag and pulled out a five wood.

Standing behind the ball, I looked down the fairway, visualising the shot before moving into position. With an easy swing I watched the ball leave the club face and finish a hundred yards from the green. I smiled inwardly before becoming lost in thought once again.

Sometimes I do miss the work routine, the satisfaction of a job well done and the interaction with all sorts of people. There was always something interesting to discuss while we toiled away. The topics ranged from the best way to cook scrambled eggs, right through to cars, sports, politics and religion. Boy, we could really end up with some heated debates over the last two.

I'm an atheist and have been for more than forty-five years. Heaven help anyone who tried to jam religion down my throat. How anyone could believe many of the stories they find in the Bible is beyond me. Knowledge is the key to the present and future, not myths.

Of course, it wasn't all chatting. Work was hard, with early starts and having to labour in all sorts of weather. Bricklayer's hands copped a belting most of the time as we couldn't wear gloves. One reason we couldn't wear gloves is because it's too bloody hot in Australia. The second reason is the hand we use to hold the brick would get caught on the stringline and slow us down. And the third reason… It's still too bloody hot! The back, neck and knees suffered excruciatingly at times and as I aged, there weren't too many days I didn't have to wear some sort of brace.

"I was an expert at repetitive strain injuries by the time I retired," I thought as I stood beside my ball once again. "A sand wedge should be perfect for this distance," I decided as I confirmed the distance to the flag.

A few seconds later the ball was sent high in the air before landing in the centre of the green. My thoughts drifted back to work as I waited for the boys to have their shots.

Invariably there would be problems of some sort on a worksite. Working with other trades could be difficult. Everyone trying to do their own jobs and all vying for the spot you are occupying. Asking someone to move their truck so you can get your gear on site could occasionally lead to blows if the blokes were having a bad day. Relying on suppliers and having to deal with supervisors who just wanted the job done regardless of rain, hail or shine, just scratched the surface of some of the issues I've had to face over the years.

I remember one time having a run in with a union representative and his goons. They hadn't wanted me to work on a particular job because of a national strike for truckies. I didn't think a government levy on trucks for damaging roads had anything to do with me, so I didn't strike. The following day I arrived at work and next thing you know, they'd overturned my cement mixer and were giving me a pretty hard time. Forty blokes surrounding my little gang of five can be fairly intimidating. What was worse, the police wouldn't do a thing. Just goes to show how powerful the unions were.

I lined up my putt and stroked it towards the hole. It teetered on the edge but wouldn't drop.

"You can have that one mate," Dave sang out.

"You don't think you're being too generous do you? After all, it's a half inch putt; I might miss," I joked, picking up the ball before he responded.

"Nah mate, you're putting pretty well today. We'll risk it," Dave taunted.

Walking to the next tee, I decided to go back to my day-dreaming rather than stew on missing a very gettable putt.

"There will be other opportunities today," I consoled myself. "Now where was I?"

All in all, I was proud of my working abilities. I knew I did a good job; the best I could and I had lots of happy clients to prove it. Word of mouth is always the best advertisement and I'd had a steady enough stream of work over the years to enable me to educate the kids, pay the house off and have a couple of rental properties. We weren't rich but we were comfortable.

I was sure our retirement years wouldn't be a hardship for us and we would be able to live the life we were accustomed to. We'd probably even manage a trip overseas once a year if we felt like it. We both liked travelling and we'd been to a few destinations, but the world was a big place and there were still plenty of areas left for us to see and explore.

I had plenty of plans for my retirement besides travelling. I was going to learn how to fly, take up lawn bowls and start those wood working projects

I'd planned ages ago. I'd already finished painting the lounge room and I'd caught up with a few odd jobs which had been bugging me for ages. I was even thinking of doing some writing classes.

"Come on, Grant! Who's away with the fairies?" Noel called. "We're only on the third hole. If you're going to take this much time we won't be finished 'til midnight."

"Okay, okay," I laughed and readied myself over the ball. Whack! Again the ball floated through the air, straight and true.

"What did you have for breakfast this morning?" Dave smiled. "Mate, you're making this a bit hard for us today."

"Don't tell me you don't like a challenge," I replied.

As Noel and Dave took their shots, I thought about how well I was playing. Mind you, every time I played was different now I was older. Golf was a funny game. You had your good days and your bad but I guess that's the way it goes with most sports.

"Today is my day," I said softly to myself, then quickly shied away from the thought. After all, I didn't want to jinx myself.

It's funny how you have your little superstitions. I knew a guy once who always wore a certain pair of underpants when he played football. Everyone rubbished him but it didn't matter. If he didn't have those undies on he played woefully. In the end, the entire team started to believe, without those undies, they didn't have a chance of winning. Before I knew it, half the team had developed some sort of phobia about what they were wearing.

Laura, on the other hand, is a numbers person. I'm not sure where she gets it from, but she believes some numbers are lucky and some aren't. For example, there is no way she would live in a house with a street address of four. The numbers can't even add up to four. Do you see how many residences get knocked out of the equation?

Number thirteen is out as one and three add up to four, as does twenty-two, thirty-one, forty, one hundred and three and one hundred and twelve. There's probably more but I can't be bothered to think about it. I would just say "Yes, dear," and move onto the next property. Why beat your head up against a brick wall?

The warm sun and a cool breeze were putting me in a happy place today and it was perfect for good golf.

"I like this hole. It's a nice, short par four," I thought as my wedge pitched the ball within eighteen inches of the flag, ensuring a certain birdie. The boys cheered and I took a bow before returning to my reveries.

I don't believe I'm superstitious in the typical way. Superstitions don't make scientific sense and are illogical to my way of thinking. I like to think my little jinx theory is more about balancing my thought processes so I don't get too emotional and risk muffing my next shot.

Anything else, like saying "Bless you," when someone sneezes, I would consider habitual good manners ingrained from my childhood days, rather than something said as a type of good luck charm for the hapless sneezer. When you come to think of it, aren't there many sayings incorporated into our language and little cultural traditions that are based on some evil befalling you, if you don't give the expected response?

Clinking glasses and drinking some of the contents immediately springs to mind. Just watch what people are like if you won't clink glasses with them. They almost take it as a personal insult. I've seen many people reluctant to walk under a ladder (at least that makes some sense), or have a black cat cross their path or spilling salt and breaking mirrors to name a few. For the worst offenders, those superstitions can actually debilitate them. Fear can do amazing things to the psyche.

Wandering over to the fourth tee after sinking my birdie putt, I steadied myself over the ball. I ran through my mental check list. Feet about shoulder width apart, grip firm but not over tight, body balanced with a little more weight on my leading foot. I did a couple of practice swings.

"Everything's okay, just keep calm and focused."

I'd only managed to bring my arm up ready for the downward swing when I felt Dave's club handle in my ribs. The shock put me off and my ball dribbled off the tee. By the time I looked around, both the guys were doubled up with laughter.

"Some mates you are," I scolded them, but I had to admit I would have done the same to one of them if the tables had been turned.

When they'd finished laughing, which seemed to take another five minutes, Noel managed to gasp, "You can have another shot."

"Too right I will, and you guys can stand way over there, near that ghost gum while I do?"

"Hey, you can trust us," they both responded in unison which set them off into fresh bouts of laughter.

"Yeah, right," I said, laughing with them.

I'm lucky having such good friends to play golf with. How many guys have pals who they have a really good relationship with? Men you could trust, who would watch your back and who you could have a joke and a good laugh with. Mind you, some of our discussions could get a bit heated and a fair bit of the old male testosterone would sometimes cause some verbal shaping up, but we'd soon get over it. I reckon it would be pretty boring if we agreed on everything one hundred percent of the time. It was good we could agree to disagree and move on.

We'd been playing golf together for over twenty years now and we'd settled into an easy routine. The starting conversation was usually about sport; rugby league, Aussie rules, cricket, you name it. Then we'd progress to our wives and families. It took up quite some time to get through how Noel's wife, Sarah and Dave's wife, Jill, were getting on and then we'd go through the various kids. By the time we'd talked about what my three, Noel's two and Dave's four were up to, we'd be half way around the golf course.

Statistically, we were in the minority. We'd all been married to our respective wives for a number of years. I still include Noel in this category even though he's been married twice. It wasn't his fault that his first wife, Meredith, had died from a melanoma. Lost in thought, I suddenly realised I'd reached my ball.

"This hole is a long par four so I'll need a three wood to get anywhere near the green," I decided.

After giving the ball a solid whack, it raced down the fairway before running into the greenside bunker on the right.

"Could be worse," I grimaced, as I returned to my reminiscences regarding Noel.

I didn't know Noel back then but it hit him really hard. They'd been married only five years. Even after all this time he'll talk about Meredith with a lump in his throat. He'll tell us what she looked like, her funny quirks, her talents and her beauty but he won't speak at all about how he felt when they found out the prognosis or how they coped until her demise. He likes to think she's an angel living happily in heaven so I don't try to disillusion him.

Sarah came along about two years after Meredith's death and obviously gave Noel a new lease on life. I believe it took Noel a while before he'd let her into his life, but Sarah's warmth, compassion and patience melted the ice that had formed around his broken heart. They've been married twenty-five years and are as settled as a pair of comfortable old shoes.

Dave's wife, Jill, is the mother earth type. She usually has plenty of kids hanging around; her own and everyone else's. Jill is friendly, placid and nothing seems to faze her. She's a great cook too. There's always something bubbling on the stove or baking in the oven and the house smells wonderful. I often wondered why Dave wasn't ten times heavier.

They'd been married thirty-one years and were just right for each other. Dave didn't mind their sometimes messy house and Jill could put up with Dave's jokes and over-the-top pranks. Their family was boisterous and rowdy but full of love and support for one another.

Our wives get on well together and will often meet up for coffee or some other social function which makes life easier for us blokes. I shudder to think of all the fun occasions we would have missed if the girls hadn't liked each other. I've heard of so many husbands and wives who seem threatened by their spouse's friends. We have been very fortunate that we've all bonded so well, kids included.

I spied my ball sitting nicely in the middle of the bunker. I chose to use a lob wedge rather than a sand wedge as I could get the ball to 'spin' and therefore stop quicker once it hit the green. The club thumped into the sand, blasting the ball out. It landed with text book style, bounced twice before skidding to a halt, ten feet short of the hole.

"Don't you love it when a plan falls into place?" I said to no-one in particular.

It probably helps our friendship that all of us men were 'tradies'. Noel was a chippy and Dave a sparky, or carpenter and electrician to anyone outside the industry. We'd helped each other out numerous times, especially at each other's houses. We'd also referred each other when the opportunity arose and someone needed a good tradesman. It really helped that we all had the same work ethic and could trust each other to fulfil our obligations to clients. That's important if you are referring someone. If they failed to do the right thing, it's a reflection on my business as well.

"Stop thinking about work in the present tense," I chided myself.

Sometimes it's difficult to believe that work is all behind me now, especially when I'm out with Dave and Noel. We just seem to naturally drift into conversation about our working days. I guess it wasn't that long ago we were out there doing the hard yards.

Dave had been the first to retire a couple of years ago, followed by Noel three months later and then me. Looking back, knowing they weren't working and were out on the golf course without me, was probably a major reason for my decision to retire.

Of course, Laura and I had discussed it many times and in great detail before I actually did the deed. I was thinking of doing one more year if Noel and Dave had continued. See, there's even peer pressure at my age. No wonder younger people often have a hard time of it.

"Time for a beer mate," Noel called, jolting me out of my reverie.

"Great! My tongue's hanging out for a coldie," I yelled back to him.

We'd decided early in our golfing partnership to limit ourselves to one drink out on the course. Not like some of the fellows who drank like fish the whole way round and ended up as dangers to themselves and anyone around them. We thought of them as the 'yobbo' golfers, usually young men who weren't that serious about the game and just wanted an excuse to booze up.

We were long past that. Sure, as I said before, we'd have a few beers after the game but we were careful not to get smashed. Let's face it; if you're married it's not only the pain from the headache you have to suffer...

It was wonderful to feel the cold, amber liquid slide down my throat. Just what the doctor ordered. The day was warming up now, not that it was ever that cold to begin with. Not like southern parts of Australia in the mornings, where I had lived all my childhood and teenage years. I shivered thinking of what golfers put themselves through to have a game down there.

Frost would make the course a glittering, icy, white spectacle, crisp and crunchy underfoot. Finding your ball in that wintry wonderland was definitely a challenge. Rugged up to the maximum, you'd watch your breath waft in the air like cigarette smoke before it gradually disappeared. Yeah, you truly had to love the game to be a southern golfer in winter.

Of course, that was nowhere near as bad as being a brickie down there. At times we had to pour petrol over the bricks and set them alight just to separate them. We had to empty the hose each afternoon because if we left water in it overnight, we couldn't use the hose again until the following afternoon.

Once I was building a wall and the mortar was freezing as I laid the bricks. Come nine o'clock, the sun hit the wall and the mortar began to melt. Bang! The wall collapsed with the weight of the bricks on the wet mortar. That's how cold winter can be in Canberra.

Tilting back my head, I finished off my beer and walked over to have my putt.

"Oh, no!" I groaned, as the all too familiar indigestion rose in my throat. "I must have drunk that beer too quickly, or the curry Laura made last night is starting to play up."

Bands of pain tightened around my chest, making me feel breathless. Reaching into my pocket, I grabbed an antacid tablet and popped it into my mouth.

I always carried antacids with me now and seemed to be using them more frequently than I would have liked. These indigestion attacks had begun about eighteen months ago and to begin with, were just minor irritations. I fobbed them off and they'd go away, but lately they were becoming more severe. Some nights I couldn't lie flat in bed and would have to walk the floor for a couple of hours.

Laura was always at me to have a doctor's check-up, but I would find excuses not to make an appointment. After all, it was only indigestion. I didn't want to sit in a room full of sick people for an hour just to be told to take some antacids which was what I was doing. I've always been a relatively healthy person. I'd had the odd cold and sinus was an ongoing problem, but that was about it; a couple of Panadols usually solved the problem.

Wiping my brow, I missed the first putt and just scraped in the second, settling for a bogey. I tried to focus on my thoughts to distract myself from the pain.

The only times I'd needed a doctor was for injuries I'd managed to sustain, mostly when I was a kid. My brother and I had an argument one day when I was about twelve. He was bigger than me, so I ended up thinking discretion was the better part of valour and I ran. I was pretty quick those days and fled into the toilet, the only room with a lockable door at our house. In his frustration, my brother threw a shoe at me just as I was closing the door. It struck the glass door panel, shattering it and a shard of glass entered my eye.

Neither of us knew what to do about it, so I lay down on my bed until our mother came home from work. Both of us were pretty subdued, worrying about how much trouble we'd be in because of the broken door. Money was tight as Mum and Dad had split up two years previously; Mum was working full time at a fruit shop to keep us with a roof over our head and food in our bellies.

I'll never forget the look on her face when she eventually arrived home and I told her what had happened. Luckily for me, I couldn't see what my eye looked like so I hadn't been overly concerned. Mum immediately ran to the neighbours and begged a lift to the hospital. I was in the operating theatre soon after.

Later on, I found out the doctor had grave concerns for my eyesight. The risk of infection was high, considering the glass was from the toilet door. If my eye became infected, there was a possibility the infection would spread and leave me completely blind. The best outcome, as far as the doctor could tell, was that I would have a 'useful' eye, an eye which could distinguish shapes and shadows but that was about all. Even then, it would be dependent on whether the stitches in my eye would hold, as they were thinner than a human hair. One rub over the next three months and the stitches would have broken. The doctor said there'd be no second chances.

After a week in hospital and countless penicillin injections jabbed in my backside, Mum was able to take me home. For the next three months, Mum stayed with me nearly every night to stop me rubbing my eye in my sleep. When the time came for my final check up with the specialist and he had removed the stitches, he was amazed.

"Your son has almost twenty-twenty vision!" he exclaimed to Mum. "I don't know how that's happened but I suggest with your luck, you should go and buy yourself a lottery ticket."

Years later I asked Mum how she'd managed to survive the marathon event of hardly any sleep of a night while still working full time every day?

"I prayed every night from the bottom of my heart," she said. "And look, my prayers were answered and you experienced a miracle."

"The miracle was the skill of the surgeon," I scoffed at her.

"But God guided his hands and gave me the strength to cope during those difficult few months," was her parting reply.

I considered it a strange reply at the time because Mum had never believed in going to church or organised religions. Even so, I guess that never stopped her believing a supernatural benefactor existed.

The boys had already teed off by the time I had walked from the green to halfway to the tee but I didn't feel up to rushing, so I just ambled along. I needed time for those antacids to kick in. I began thinking about some of the other times I'd been crook during my life time.

At thirteen or fourteen I couldn't seem to keep out of hospital. I'd broken my leg twice in six months about a year after my eye accident. The following year, I was back in for a tonsillectomy. I was so sick of hospitals by this stage that I checked myself out of hospital the day after the operation and caught the bus home. Boy, didn't that caused a ruckus. But I still wouldn't go back to the hospital.

I'd missed so much school that every time I made an appearance, they thought I was a new student and with the lack of activity, I put on a lot of weight. I didn't start losing any of it until two years later when, at the age of sixteen, I started work.

I gripped my club and swung it but my hands were wet and clammy and the ball shot into the rough. Perspiration beaded on my forehead and my jaw ached.

"Bad luck mate," Dave commiserated. "What happened? Did the pressure of all those good shots get to you? Couldn't keep it up anymore, huh?" he teased me.

"I'll make it up next shot, as soon as I get the ball out of the rough," I said, hiding my discomfort.

I walked slowly to my waiting ball and chipped it out of the long grass onto the middle of the fairway. The effort made me feel nauseous and I leant against a tree, trying to ease the tight band of pain around my chest. I felt as if an elephant was sitting on me, squeezing the breath out of my lungs.

Rejoining the guys, I tried to take my mind off myself and concentrate on their banter. The two of them were chattering away like magpies, talking about a dreadful earthquake and tsunami which had recently occurred in Japan.

"It must be utter hell over there for those poor sods," Noel was saying.

"Yeah," Dave replied. "What could go wrong has gone wrong. Who could imagine what it would feel like to have a major earthquake, a giant tsunami, a nuclear meltdown and be homeless in the middle of winter with no shelter, food and clean water or heating?"

"Just awful," I muttered, trying to join in.

At the sound of my voice both men looked at me.

"Are you all right Grant?" Noel asked, concern written all over his face. "You look positively grey."

"Are you sure you don't want to sit down mate?" Dave said gruffly, not sure what to do.

"No, no, I'll be okay," I managed to tell them. "I've just got a really bad case of indigestion. I'll be fine once we get back to the club and sit down for another beer," I joked feebly.

I didn't want them to worry about me, so I gathered my last reserves of strength, finished the fifth hole and headed stoically to the sixth. I managed to get my tee shot away and stagger to the green. By this time the pain was so intense I could hardly bear it. The agony filled my chest, back and jaw and shot down my left arm. I picked up my club and shakily putted the ball toward the hole.

As soon as the ball began to roll, the pain exploded in my chest. I could feel my hands loosening their grip and the club dropped to my side. My knees buckled and I felt myself falling face first. I felt nothing as I hit the ground.

Suddenly, I saw my body lying there with Noel and Dave tugging at me, before turning my body over. I heard Noel's frantic calling of my name and saw other golfers running toward us as Dave desperately cried for help. I watched as Noel tried to breathe air into my lungs and Dave started compressions on my chest.

"Silly git," I thought. "Noel, buddy, you are never going to get air into anyone's lungs without tilting their head back."

They tried hard, I can tell you that. They didn't give up for one second until the paramedics arrived to take over. I watched dispassionately as my body was placed on a stretcher and loaded into a waiting ambulance. Tears streamed down Noel's face as he climbed in beside me. I heard him tell Dave to break the news to Laura. Then there was nothing but blackness...

CHAPTER II

I have no idea how long I was unconscious. I only remember waking to a soft, silvery female voice coaxing me from my black cocoon of oblivion. All I could see were two small, twinkling lights a few inches apart at around chest height. There was an upside down U-shaped band just above the twinkling lights. Both were multi-coloured, like some sort of glittering rainbow above two glorious stars, though even more striking than one could imagine. I gazed at the splendour of the colours, spellbound for minutes (or was it hours?)

I gradually started to become more aware of what the liquid voice was saying. It appeared the owner of the voice knew me for I could hear the whisper of my name floating through my head.

"Where am I?"

"You are in the Afterlife," I heard her say.

"What in the hell is the Afterlife?" I wanted to yell, thinking that's what most people would do in this situation, but I felt too calm.

Did I really care?

"Yes," I convinced myself. "You need to know what's happening, Grant. You've never shied away from knowledge your entire life. This is definitely not the time to start now," I decided as I forced myself to waken.

37

"What is the Afterlife?" I asked suspiciously.

"The Afterlife is the place of all understanding."

"Well, that's great," I thought to myself, because at the moment I'm not understanding much at all.

"Where is this Afterlife?"

"The Afterlife is in everything and encompasses all things," she calmly replied.

"Who are you?"

"I am called Niara."

"Where are you, Niara? I can't see you."

"I am before you Grant. You are looking at me."

Puzzled, I suddenly realised that the beautiful lights appeared to be the source of the voice.

"Who are you? What are you?"

"I am your guide, Grant. I will assist you. As for what I am, I am part of the Creator, just as you are."

This wasn't making sense. I decided I definitely needed more information.

"Let's start from the beginning," I demanded. "What exactly is the Afterlife again?"

"The Afterlife is where you must learn. It is part of the Creator's plan. You must discover your purpose."

"And you're going to help me do that, right?" I asked her.

"In a way," she responded mysteriously.

"That was a simple question. Can't you just tell me yes or no?"

"It is not for me to help as you define help, but to show you the way."

"But where am I going?"

"Everywhere and nowhere," was the dreamy reply.

This was all getting too much for me. I almost felt like I was Alice in Wonderland at the Madhatter's tea party!

"You're not making sense," I grumbled. "What's happened to me?"

"You have passed on Grant."

"What are you talking about? What have I passed on?"

"Your Aura has passed on, your inner energy."

"Well I hate to break it to you love, but I haven't passed anything on and I feel fine."

"I am pleased to hear that Grant," and her voice trailed off.

I waited a while to see if this rainbow was going to say something else.

Finally I asked, "Are you still there?"

"Yes Grant, I am still here."

"Well, what do we do now?"

"We wait until you are ready."

"Wait until I'm ready for what?"

"We will wait until you are ready to accept the fact you are no longer with the living."

"I'm sure if you saw it from my point of view, your perception of a fact and my perception of a fact are completely different. Perhaps you need to go to a church to find the kind of people you're looking for? They love this sort of nonsense."

"It appears you require me to be blunt. Very well; you are dead Grant," Niara responded.

"Well, if I'm dead how can I be talking to you?" I asked triumphantly, sure she would see the logic in this.

"You do not understand, Grant. You have left your body. You are not alive, you just ARE. When the time comes you will understand."

Now I was sure I was dreaming. How else could I be seeing and hearing this strange creature with her nonsensical propositions?

"I know what happened," I thought to myself. "I bet I'm in hospital in an induced coma. I was obviously still alive to be able to experience Dave and Noel working on me albeit from the strange angle of being above. That was probably my mind playing tricks because of the lack of oxygen. No, they must have succeeded in getting me going again and now I'm recovering."

I felt better for having worked this out. Since this was just a dream, I decided the best idea for now was just to go with the flow until I woke up.

"Anyway," I thought to myself, "at least this is an interesting dream and my imagination is still working. With a bit of luck this dream will show I haven't suffered any brain damage."

"Are there any more like you around here?" I joked.

"Yes," Niara stated. "There are many, although each aura is different, just as snowflakes are different. You are quite faint presently but you will become clearer as you progress. I will show you how you appear at this moment."

Shocked, I saw an image reflected off what I don't know, but I realised somehow I was seeing me as I now was. My mind reeled as I looked and saw two twinkling lights with the same multi-hued band, paler and more indistinct than Niara, but definitely there.

"What is this?" I wondered. "If this was some sort of dream, why did it seem so real that it would actually shock me?"

I started to feel anxious so I pressed the question.

"Niara, am I dreaming?" I asked while desperately willing her to say yes.

Instead I received a gentle "No."

"You are not dreaming, Grant. You need to accept that you are in the Afterlife. If not, we will wait. Time is irrelevant here. "

"But I don't want to be dead."

Actually, if this was death, it wasn't all that bad I decided. It's just that while I was alive I'd feared death so much it had become habitual not to want to be in that state. Still, it wasn't making total sense so I wasn't going without a fight.

"I don't believe you!" I screamed. "I am not dead and I AM dreaming!"

"Grant, it appears you require proof of your demise and transition into the Afterlife," Niara gently conceded.

"Damn straight I do!"

I still believed there was nothing she could say or do which I wouldn't be able to explain away by imagining my own subconscious thoughts were dreaming the whole thing up.

"You believe there is nothing I can say or do that you can't explain by your subconscious thoughts dreaming the whole thing up. That is what you are thinking now Grant."

I was too stunned to answer immediately so all Niara got was some "ums" and "ahs." My mind was racing. If my subconscious was quick-witted enough to devise a plan of proof by telling me what I was thinking, why couldn't it come back with an equally fast retort for my side of the argument?

"Yes Niara, I...I do believe that," I stumbled.

"And now you are confused why your subconscious is quick-witted for me and slow for you," Niara probed.

"I... I don't know what to think. Something happened on the golf course and I'm completely confused at the moment. I probably just need more rest but for some reason my mind isn't allowing me. This MUST be a DREAM! There is no such thing as an AFTERLIFE!"

"I will let you rest and dispel your doubts at the same time," whispered Niara.

"Yeah, well that works well for me. As long as I don't have to think too hard and I can rest, you go for your life."

"Relax and listen Grant. Your final proof begins."

The music softly enveloped me. Music I had never heard or experienced in my life. It felt alive and tangible, so uplifting that I was sure I'd drifted up to the stratosphere. With my eyes closed, incredibly I could smell and taste the flavours of a rainbow. It was breathtaking. One moment it felt as if I was soaring through the clouds like an eagle and the next the clouds would envelop me like a new-born babe wrapped in cotton wool. I had never experienced such utter joy and complete security in all my years. I wished it would never stop and would cocoon me forever. This was the highest of highs and unimaginable bliss.

Eventually the music faded and finally ceased. I felt like crying because of the sheer beauty of the experience and I longed for its return. Niara was right. There could be no doubt left in me and there was only one conclusion left. I had to face the harsh reality that I had died. There was no music like that in existence on Earth or in my subconscious.

"You win Niara," was all I could choke out.

After recovering from the shocking realisation I hadn't survived my heart attack and was actually dead, I became aware my stance as an atheist had been way out of the ball park. There shouldn't be an Afterlife. It was ridiculous! I was having trouble wrapping my head around the fact I'd been wrong all my life. I'd been mistaken about what happened before, during and after death.

How could I have possibly got it so wrong; made such drastic errors? Nothing had given me cause to think it would be remotely like this ... whatever this was. I was distressed at my failure to comprehend and analyse this eventuality. I felt let down by my powers of reasoning and intellectual ability before my death.

This reality had me more at sea than any of the events which had so far occurred. I'd relied on my brain and logic to make sense of the world. Without that one hundred percent assurance of reliable thought processes leading to a correct assumption, I grappled to keep my sanity. How can I accept being wrong all my life about something so illogical? It was almost a relief to hear Niara tell me she was leaving.

"When will you be back?"

"When you have had time to settle and come to terms with yourself," she said kindly. "Do not be too hard on yourself, Grant. There are many things you still do not know."

With that, she faded from my view and I was left alone with my thoughts. I decided then and there that I would have to go on a self-analysis journey to discover how I could have been so wrong. There must have been clues I had missed along the way!

"At least it's quiet now Niara's gone and I can rest," I contemplated.

Silence, silence so complete it was unimaginable and blackness beyond comparison. My mind started to drift, struggling for a way to find safe ground. In my semi-conscious state I started to recall a time, a time when it was quiet like this. It was long ago when I was a young man...

Laura and I had made a couple of trips to Uluru, the first time before we were married. Uluru was called Ayers Rock then and we were there just a few months before Azaria Chamberlain was taken by a dingo. That was world news as Azaria was just nine weeks old. The parents were accused of murdering her. After three trials and Azaria's mother spending three years in jail, they were finally acquitted.

We were able to camp very close to the Rock and the dingoes were everywhere. They were quite fearless and would wander through the campsite looking for scraps of food. After Azaria died, they shot every single dingo they could find within fifty miles and that amounted to hundreds of dingoes. I felt sorry for the dingoes because it was people feeding them which created the problem in the first place, by making them fearless. As sorry as I felt for the dingoes, it was incomparable to the Chamberlain's loss.

We made our second trip when our eldest daughter Casey, worked there as a tour guide. The evenings spent out in the desert in our tents were the best part of the whole experience for me. I had never heard such solitude before. Not a frog croaked or a bird chirped. The silence seemed endless, hauntingly unique.

The silence I was now experiencing in the Afterlife was three times more profound as I peered into the depthless darkness.

My thoughts strayed to the rest of that trip. Casey had loved her work there and had soaked up information about the area like a sponge. Laura and I were very impressed when we went on a tour which Casey had conducted. Knowledge spouted from her mouth in a flow of facts, stories and traditions about the terrain and the Indigenous people of the area.

Maybe it was the talk of life after death with Niara that started it, but I found myself remembering the Creation story that Casey had related from the Aboriginal people. I recalled how riveted everyone on the coach had been as she began.

"Once, everything was still. Only the Father of All Spirits was awake. He gently woke up the Sun Mother. As she awoke, a warm ray of light spread out towards the Earth.

"The Father of All Spirits said to her, 'Mother, I have work for you. Go down to the Earth and give the sleeping spirits forms.' The Sun Mother came to the Earth which was bare and everywhere she walked, plants grew. She returned to where she had begun and rested, very pleased with herself. The Father of All Spirits wanted her to do more and told her to go into the caves to wake the spirits there.

"The Sun Mother went inside and the bright light which emanated from her awoke the spirits and they became all kinds of insects. The Sun Mother was very happy to see the insects mingling with the beautiful flowers. However, the Father urged her to do still more.

"Finding a very deep cave the Sun Mother ventured inside and spread her light around. Her radiant heat melted the ice and all the rivers and streams of the world were produced. She created all the small snakes, frogs, lizards and fish and then all the birds in an array of gorgeous colours. The Father of All Spirits was very pleased. The Mother gathered her creatures to her and told them to enjoy all the wealth of the earth and to live in harmony with one another. She left them then and rose into the sky to become the sun.

"All the creatures watched in awe and amazement as the sun inched her way across the sky towards the west. When she finally sank below the horizon, they were terrified at the thought she had deserted them. Frozen with fear, they stood throughout the night thinking that the end of time had come. After what seemed an eternity, the Sun Mother finally peeked over the rim of the Earth to the East. Eventually, the creatures adapted to the coming and going of the sun and were no longer afraid.

"To begin with, peace filled the earth but over time envy crept into the hearts of the children of the earth. They fought and argued, so the Sun Mother left her place in the sky and came to mediate between them. She gave the animals the power to change their form to whatever they desired, but she was very displeased with the end results.

"Some of her beautiful rats had changed into bats and there were lizards with blue tongues and giant fish. The strangest of the new animals had a bill like a duck, a tail like a beaver, a mammal's body but was able to lay eggs. It called itself a platypus. The Sun Mother began to fear the Father of All Spirits would be angered when he saw these new animals, so she decided she would create new creatures.

"She gave birth to two children; the Morning Star god and the Moon goddess. They produced two children and these two were sent to the Earth. They were made superior to the animals because they had part of the Sun Mother's mind and would never want to change their shape. They were our ancestors."

I don't know why that story stuck in my mind but it had. At the time, I had understood how the Aborigines could come up with a tale like that. The huge shape of Uluru jutting from the ground, the red soil, the hazy heat and their amazing capacity to live from a land which was totally inhospitable to visitors would surely have them dreaming of a way to explain the existence of the things surrounding them.

"This Afterlife place I now find myself in might be considered inhospitable. The complete darkness, the eerie silence, could be thought creepy. Yet I don't have that feeling at all," I mused.

That wasn't the only story Casey told that day to explain the Creation from the viewpoint of the original settlers. Our girl had a talent for making people feel as if they were part of the story. I felt like I was there, listening to the guttural voices of the elders as they sat around a campfire in the dark of night, relating the ancient stories to their children, as Casey began.

"In the Dreamtime, all the Earth lay sleeping. Nothing moved or grew until one day the Rainbow Serpent awoke and came out from under the ground. She travelled over the Earth, leaving tracks and marks from her body. Eventually, she called for the frogs to come out and join her.

"They came slowly as their bellies were filled with water which had stored there while they were sleeping. The Rainbow Serpent tickled their stomachs and when the frogs laughed, the water from inside them filled the tracks and holes the Rainbow Serpents body had made, forming lakes and rivers.

"Once water filled the Earth, plants and trees grew and then all the animals awoke. They were happy and each type of animal lived with his own tribe, gathering the food that suited them. Some of the animals lived in the air, some in the rocks and others on the plains.

"The Rainbow Serpent made laws that all were to obey but eventually some of the animals became quarrelsome. As a reward for good behaviour, the serpent promised that those who obeyed would be given human form but those who disobeyed would be turned to stone, never again to walk the Earth.

"Disbelieving, there were some who broke the laws and they were turned to stone and became the mountains and hills. The obedient ones were given human form and a totem of the animals they once were. Each tribe knew themselves by their totem. There were many totems but some of them were kangaroo, carpet snake and emu.

"To ensure no-one would starve and there would be plenty of food for all, the Rainbow Serpent decreed that no tribe was to eat from its own totem, only the animals belonging to other tribe's totems. The tribes lived contentedly on the land given to them by the Serpent, safe in the knowledge the land would always be theirs and never taken from them."

Yes, those stories made an impact on me and I realised there was often a common thread in many religious and ancient stories. In Christianity, Genesis talks of "In the beginning..." and the land being a formless waste. Creatures are created and the life force or spirit of God is given to them so they are alive. A serpent is mentioned along with rules which result in a reward for obedience or punishment for disobedience. Peace was the original concept for how mankind should live together. American Indians, Hindus, Muslims and many others all had similar stories.

I explained it to myself using some information I'd heard about, a phenomena known as the 'Hundredth monkey syndrome'. Apparently there is a group of small islands somewhere in the world where scientists had been studying the monkey populations over a period of time. Each island group was in isolation.

One female on an island learnt how to wash the sand from her food. Gradually, from observing her, other monkeys on the island also began washing their food. What stunned the scientists though was that the monkeys on the other islands also started washing their food without anyone teaching them.

A theory evolved that once there are enough living creatures knowing something, the knowledge somehow becomes universal. To me, this was a plausible explanation for a host of so-called 'unexplainable' instances where people have obtained information which, technically, they shouldn't have been privy to. I kind of liked the idea I was linked into a network of human thought, part of a global think tank.

I'd envisioned we were all like herd animals and had an inherent need to be connected to one another. My idea was that it was a survival instinct which made us strive to join together, much like a herd of wildebeest when a pride of lions is nearby. United we stand, divided we fall.

Now though, I was all out of whack with my thoughts and I didn't know what to believe anymore. I kept hearing Niara saying 'You are not alive, you just ARE.' What exactly did that mean? What purpose did I have? What did I have to learn? What was I if I wasn't something living?

For the first time in my life I felt there were things beyond my comprehension and the thought frightened me immeasurably. The whole idea of being wrong about so many things undermined my belief in myself and completely negated any joy I might have felt at having some sort of 'existence' after death.

"I should be feeling, at the very least, somewhat relieved," I told myself. "I'm still thinking and I have memories. That's a start."

CHAPTER III

I started to think back on what had made me believe the things I did. Around the age of fifteen, I developed a fascination for the theory of evolution, particularly hominid evolution and astronomy. I was an avid reader and read every book I could lay my hands on regarding those two subjects.

I devoured 'On the Origin of Species' by Charles Darwin, 'Unveiling Man's Origins' by Louis Leakey and 'The Character of Physical Law' by Richard Feynmann. I sailed through 'Chariots of the Gods' by Erich von Daniken which was hugely popular around that time, though not particularly scientific. I'd always been curious and wouldn't accept anything at face value. I usually had to test every statement which drove my childhood family insane.

Even Dr. Wheeler, the surgeon who had saved my eyesight, commented to my mother on my questioning regarding the procedure and expected outcomes.

"I have never come across a child who asks such in-depth and relevant questions," he told Mum. "He asks questions that most adults don't ask me."

I prided myself on my knowledge and wasn't slow to defend what I had learnt, especially when I came across people espousing a God who was responsible for the creation of the Earth and all things upon it. Their attempts to convert me to their way of thinking fell on deaf ears.

I'd tell them of all the books I had read which supported my belief system and numbered in the hundreds by the time I reached twenty. They only had the Bible to back their claims. Patiently, I'd explain the logic behind the theory of evolution and why they were wrong.

"Haven't you heard of the term 'Natural Selection'?" I'd ask. "Darwin used the phrase 'survival of the fittest,' not necessarily describing the most robust creature but the creature which fitted its environment the best. Every living thing which adapts itself to a particular environment has the best chance of survival. Hence, if the environment changes for whatever reason, only the creatures which evolve in response to that change will survive. The ones who do not adapt die out.

"Humans have used artificial selection for thousands of years, creating all the different varieties of sheep, cattle, horses, dogs, cats, pigeons and so forth. They have managed to do that by carefully choosing a particular trait in animals and breeding them with animals which have the same or similar trait. Either that or they just dispose of the litter of the offspring which doesn't carry the desired characteristic. By continually breeding back to the desired requirement, the trait becomes firmly established as a new breed.

"In the deserts of Syria, Sheik Mirza the second, a Fedan Bedouin, owned a bay Arab colt which caught the eye of the British Consul, Thomas Darley. Darley paid the Sheik three hundred gold sovereigns for the yearling and impatiently waited for delivery, only to find the Sheik had second thoughts and declared he couldn't possibly part with his finest colt. Darley, not to be deprived, made arrangements with some sailors and smuggled the horse out via Smyrna, eventually arriving in England with him in 1704.

"Ninety five percent of all modern Thoroughbred racehorses can be traced to this single stallion. Line breeding with the Darley Arabian and two other stallions, the Godolphin Arabian and the Byerley Turk and some selected mares, account for virtually all the Thoroughbreds.

"In nature, the exact same process occurs except randomly. No-one is choosing what the end product will become. Given enough time and changing environments, animals will evolve into quite extreme variations. You only have to look at the variation which occurs within the canine species to understand what I mean. Yes, I know most dog breeds have been artificially selected by humans, but just imagine what could have happened naturally if all dogs had been left to their own devices.

"The fact you can have dogs as diverse as a Great Dane, a Poodle, an English Bulldog and a Chihuahua, all originally produced from a wolf, proves my point that animals can change quite radically with minor mutations. After a few million years, with many more minor mutations, it wouldn't require too much imagination to see a new species emerge that looked nothing like a dog.

"Mutations can change the way something adapts to its environment, perhaps making an organism stronger or faster or bigger. When eyes evolved at the start of the Cambrian period about six hundred million years ago, it created mutations and new species at such an incredible rate that the period is described as the Cambrian explosion. With the advent of eyes, predators became much more mobile. Prey required much better protection. Mutations, such as scales or hard shells, all came about during that time period, in response to animals being able to see for the first time in history.

"Of course, one of the best known transitional species is Archaeopteryx, a half bird, half dinosaur which was thought to have lived about one hundred and fifty million years ago. It had the head and legs of a small dinosaur, teeth, feathered wings and a bony tail covered with long feathers.

"Archaeopteryx was such a perfect example of a dinosaur transitioning to some type of bird that even scientists at the time thought it must be a hoax. After many more of these creatures were unearthed, the hoax theories were dispelled."

I remembered at the time of my death, scientists had just discovered what they thought could be a new transitional species and science wasn't sure where to put Archaeopteryx. Was it still a transitional species, a very strange bird or an unusual type of dinosaur? I supposed only time would tell.

Now I didn't know what to believe. I was wrong about the existence of an Afterlife and wrong about a Creator. Is it possible I was wrong about everything? Could science have dropped the ball that badly that everything I had believed in was false? I needed to reflect and churn over events in my past. Find out where I went wrong.

The thing I'd loved about those subjects back then was that all the experts in their field were vying for their place in the sun. No dogma or theory was safe, not even sacred Archaeopteryx could escape the relentless search for the truth. Each theory would be checked and re-checked and only accepted if it couldn't be proven otherwise, or some new discovery supported it. Like a giant jigsaw puzzle, just when you thought you had the right piece in the right place, science would discover at a later date that another similar piece went there instead. It wasn't safe like religion but it was exciting and you could question it.

Alas, all my wonderful arguments came to nought when discussing them with a religious person.

"Grant, can't you just look around you and see that all this diversity can't just be random. That there is order in everything and therefore there must be someone who designs all these things, just as the Bible says," I would hear them respond.

"Yes, we agree species can change by adapting to their environment. They adapt by evolving some attribute which helps ensure their survival but they do not change from the 'kind' of animal that they originally started from. There is no scientific or scriptural evidence to indicate a fish can become a cat or an amoeba can become an elephant, no matter how many millions of years pass. There is only a theory which says this has occurred and can occur.

"And after all, this theory still doesn't explain how life came to be on this planet to begin with or how the Universe started. The Bible tells us that a Supreme Being, a dynamic energy source with the ability to know all things, created us and the Earth and everything upon it. How is that harder to believe than a primeval soup occurring which somehow managed to produce a single cell that split enough times to change and alter into everything we see on this planet today?"

They could go on and on and on, but then again so could I. I would eventually walk away, never understanding how they could be so blind.

"Now it appears I was the blind one. All those silly arguments," I thought, berating myself. "And I never gave up either," recalling the solution I came up with to beat them at their own game.

I'd teach these Bible bashers a lesson they would never forget. I was determined to find as many faults as I could to prove it was their book that was wrong. I felt if I could find just one single, major flaw in a book which was supposedly guided by the hand of God, then all their arguments would be meaningless because the Bible couldn't be wrong.

I started reading the New Testament and it nearly convinced me to never read a book again. It was so boring. It took me six months to doggedly plough through that one book. I couldn't understand why they felt the need to tell the same story four times and two of those stories almost word for word. Obviously plagiarism wasn't illegal back then. Towards the end, I was struggling to get through five pages per week. And sadly, I wasn't getting too much ammunition.

After a few months of recovery I decided to tackle the Old Testament. Talk about hitting pay dirt! It was a gold mine of ammunition. It appeared to me that every ten pages the book contradicted itself. 'Thou shalt not kill' was a classic example. You either had God himself exterminating thousands or you had him ordering his chosen people to invade cities and slaughter every man, woman and child.

'Thou shalt not commit adultery' was the next one. Why would any guy want to commit adultery when it was perfectly acceptable for him to have multiple wives, concubines and slave girls? And how about 'Love thy neighbour,' where you're able to keep slaves and even beat them to death? And as long as they didn't die straight away, you didn't even have to part with any shekels of silver for retribution.

'Do not covet thy neighbours' wife.' Yeah, sure. So why did God give all of King David's wives to his neighbours when David had committed adultery with Bathsheba? Surely that means God was encouraging David's neighbours to covet David's wives and also commit adultery? Go figure!

The amazing thing about that story was, in the end, David wasn't severely punished. No, the one who appeared to be punished was David's innocent baby boy. He was the one God chose to kill. And here we are again at 'Thou shalt not kill.' I just couldn't make sense of it.

The more I read, the more contradictions I found. One minute they would be saying 'turn the other cheek' and the next minute it would be 'an eye for an eye'. God is called a merciful God and yet he would smote some of his followers, destroy entire cities, turn a woman to salt because she looked behind her, or ordering the Israelites to show no mercy to the inhabitants of the cities they were invading. The list seemed endless.

"No wonder there are so many different factions in Christianity," I remember thinking. "No-one could make head or tail of this and come up with an answer which everyone would agree with. How would anyone know the correct path to follow?"

"Were any of these paths the one I was supposed to follow? How could I have possibly chosen any of them?" I thought. "Keep on searching Grant."

I started to enjoy myself when I got to the section relating to Moses' ancestry right back to Adam and Eve. I realised all I had to do was add up how long each ancestor had lived for, according to the Bible and I'd have the exact year the Earth and the Universe were created. Within an hour I'd worked out the date to 4004 B.C. To me this was incredible information. No sane person could possibly believe the Earth and the Universe could only be six thousand years old. There are trees thought to be older than that.

Many years later I read an article about someone who had done the same computations as me, albeit hundreds of years earlier and he'd been touted as some sort of genius. I was certainly no genius and to me it was just simple mathematics and logic, but I was pleased we'd both arrived at the same date.

Regrettably for me, in the 1960s and 1970s, many of the Christian factions were trying to fit in with science, so to extend the age of the six thousand years, they began to say the days of Creation were not six literal twenty-four hour periods but a day of undetermined length such as when we might use the term 'day' in the sentence 'In his day...,' meaning generation. Another thought was that a day to God could represent a thousand years or a million years. Drat, cheated again!

Funnily enough, some years later after the Churches started losing their patrons by the truckload, partly for being too confusing and partly for being hypocritical, most of them reverted back to fundamentalism and the Creation days returned to being a literal twenty-four hour period. How bizarre is that? In the meantime, I had to wait to shoot my newfound ammunition into the hearts of religious men and women. Strangely though, one thing my arguments never did was convince one person I was right and they were wrong. In all my years I never converted one religious person.

"Now that I'm up here it's probably a good thing I wasn't successful in converting anyone," I reflected. "Perhaps I should have done more listening and less talking."

Thinking about religion reminded me of a guy I met when I was in my early teens named Steven. Steve ended up having a profound influence on my life. He was a Christian, but he never spoke about it back then.

I met Steven when he started bringing homework to my house when I had all my accidents. After I had recovered and put on a heap of weight, he must have decided it was up to him to try and remove some of that fat. One day he came over and asked if I would like to go for a run around the oval with him. The oval was a sports field about half a mile away.

I thought, "This kid is nuts! Why would anyone actually choose to run around in circles when everyone else is trying to avoid running around in circles?"

I graciously declined his kind invitation. However, he was a persistent little blighter and after a few months of his pestering, I finally agreed and started running with him.

One time we took a football and my dog with us. This dog was very savage and played rough. We were mucking around and Steve ended up lying on top of the football. Well, my dog obviously thought he wasn't playing fair so he bit Steve really hard on the backside. Steve let out a scream so long and loud I was certain the dog had ripped his testicles off. He was writhing on the ground in agony. After I saw the size of the bite on his bum, bleeding and already black and blue, I had a better understanding of why he'd screamed so loudly!

That dog sure was fierce but he was the smartest dog I've ever come across. He was a border collie cross we'd named Shadow and just about anything we ever taught him only took one attempt to learn. Sit, lie down, shake hands and roll over were all learnt within a few minutes. You could hold out your arms and he would leap into them. If you wanted a cuddle, all you needed to do was drop to your knees and say,

"Shadow, give me a cuddle."

He would put a paw on each shoulder and rest his chin beside your neck. If he wasn't in the mood to cuddle, he might growl softly in your ear just to put the wind up you. If we wanted him to guard something, we would instruct him by saying,

"Look after this, Shadow."

You could come back hours later and the dog would still be there. If someone got too close, he would put both paws on the object in question, bare his teeth and give the most ferocious, blood curdling growls you have ever heard. If you were stupid enough to try and grab it, say goodbye to some skin and blood.

It became one of our mother's favourite party tricks when we were in our late teens. Any of the guys who brought beer were told to leave it in the middle of the lounge room floor and they would wonderingly do as they were told. Then Mum would put Shadow on guard.

"Just making sure you don't drink too much," she'd tell them wickedly.

Funny that, we never did have any drunks at our house, though there were quite a few punctured beer cans.

"Thinking about those beer cans has made me realise I haven't needed to drink yet. I guess not having a body means nourishment isn't required. Do I need anything?" I wondered, before thinking about Shadow again.

The best trick Shadow ever learnt, surprisingly he taught himself. One day we were out in the yard with a group of kids playing hide and seek. The dog kept finding the children and giving away their hiding places; so we put him inside the house. Mum was doing the laundry and observed Shadow watching the children as they ran in and out of the house through the laundry door.

Apparently, Shadow just sat staring at that door. He didn't budge, in fact hardly moved a muscle, so intent was he in watching the way people opened and closed the door. After about the fifth time someone had gone in and out, Shadow walked over to the door, stood on his hind legs, put one paw on the latch and pulled down as the other paw was pushing the door open.

Once he'd learnt to open doors there was no stopping him. Again, a simple instruction was all that was required to get him to open or close a door.

"Shadow, close the door."

He'd walk over and hook his paw behind the door if it was opened right up to the wall. When the gap was large enough to accommodate him, he would stand on his hind legs behind the door and push it until it closed.

He never mastered the art of opening doors with round handles but he used to give it a good try. He'd put both paws on either side of the handle and twist. He could get it to a quarter turn but never quite enough to fully disengage the lock. Yeah, he was a smart dog alright. You could learn lessons from him, not only about things he'd work out, but also about unconditional love and loyalty.

The best lesson I ever learnt about loyalty didn't come from the dog though. No, that lesson came from Steve at my sister Keira's twenty-first birthday party, when Steve and I were about eighteen. I'd invited a girl who I'd recently met to be my date, but as soon as we'd arrived I was sequestered into doing some bar work which left my date on her own and free to get up to her own devices. She took one look at Steve's lithe, muscled body and must have thought, "That will do me."

Jumping into a secluded broom closet, she beckoned Steve to follow her. Now Steve wasn't much of a talker back then, more a man of action. Without a word he walked over, reached in, grabbed her by the arm and yanked her so hard her feet nearly left the floor. Then he just walked away. You know, I learnt more about loyalty from that single action than if I'd read a dozen books on the subject.

"I wonder how loyal Niara is going to be? Perhaps she's just the welcoming party and there will be other rainbow people guiding me as well? No-one else seems to be very interested in checking on me too often. But that suits me fine," I decided. "I need lots of time to think."

My teenage years seemed to be a whirlwind of activity. I left school at sixteen and started a bricklaying apprenticeship, working from dawn 'til dusk six days a week. I'd been heavily involved with riding horses until then, but I still managed to get out to them on weekends and occasionally after work in summer.

My brother and I had more than one hundred pets where we lived on a small suburban block and they all needed time and attention. There were pigeons, ducks, chooks, turkeys, parrots, rabbits, guinea pigs, ferrets, quails, bantams, magpies, dogs and cats. We even kept a horse there for a short time. My brother made it into the local newspaper once with the heading, 'Richard chasing Noah's record.' It used to take at least an hour a day just to feed, water and clean their cages. How our mother coped with all the noise, mess and various disasters which happen when you have a whole backyard of differing animals beats me.

In my spare time I played tennis and ran eight kilometres twice a week. I'd go out with my mates once a week and rarely drank alcohol. I saw my girlfriend only once a week as well. In hindsight, I realise she must have truly loved me to put up with that sort of treatment. I can't imagine any girl putting up with that nowadays.

By the time I was nineteen I'd started my Clerk of Works course and bought a forty acre block of rural land with Richard. We were heartily sick of agistment fees for our growing herd of mares and geldings. Both of us were rapt with everything pertaining to horses. Apart from riding and taking them to gymkhanas, we bred them and broke the young ones in ourselves.

There were plenty of bumps, bruises, kicks and falls during that period. Possibly the worst injury I sustained was a bite on my chest from a stallion I was working with. Those great, white, square teeth clamping down on my bare flesh imparted agony like you wouldn't believe. Because the skin is so taut in the chest area for a male, there wasn't a lot the doctors could do for me in the way of stitches or anything. It took a couple of weeks before I could even stand up straight.

When I was twenty, Richard and I bought a four bedroom house together in a quiet, leafy, older suburb of Canberra. We moved in with our mother, her cockatoo, some pigeons and the dog and cat. We'd managed to whittle down the rest of our menagerie in the previous year. I look back now and wonder how I'd managed to fit everything in?

I had no idea how long it had been since Niara left and I'd started contemplating my life. Obviously though, enough time had passed for my brain (brain?) to adjust and at least my mind wasn't spinning like it had been. I started reflecting on Niara's words to me. I still didn't know what I had to learn and what my purpose was going to be. Deep in thought, I churned ideas around and around in my head.

The music started playing again, so gentle and soft, massaging my tortured mind. It seemed to start whenever my energy was ebbing to a low point. Strangely, on Earth I was never fussed on massages. For some reason it made me feel vulnerable.

"If they had something like this down there, it would've been a totally different story. I would have had one every day!"

CHAPTER IV

Niara's soft voice startled me from my reverie. "Are you feeling rested Grant?"

"Yes I am and thanks for asking. I was beginning to wonder if you were ever coming back."

"Grant, I am never far away. You need time to recover and adjust before you start the first phase of your journey."

"Oh really, and what is the first phase of my journey, pray tell?"

"It is time to start learning how to adjust in a world without bodies. Where you are now is in a vacuum of space. This means there are no forces acting on you. So there is no gravity, no wind, no objects, nothing."

With me listening intently now, she continued.

"To move, you will actually have to project yourself there. It can be very daunting and difficult at first," she warned. "You will need to pinpoint an exact spot and totally convince yourself that you are there. With practice you will gain confidence. Once you truly believe, it becomes very simple."

"Are you sure I can do this?"

"Yes, Grant. You must learn to do this. There is no other way," she stated firmly. "It will be entirely up to you though how long it will take."

"How long does it usually take?" I asked her, feeling a bit nervous about what her response would be.

"A day, a million days, the length of time is irrelevant. What is important is that you learn."

"There's that learning again," I groaned.

I don't have a problem with learning if I just knew what I was learning and what for. I like to know what the big picture is.

"Niara, am I learning to do this to get out of here?"

"It is more than that Grant. You are learning so you may become part of here," was her strange reply.

Every time I asked Niara something she'd make my head start spinning again. If I wasn't part of where I was now, how was I going to be part of it by moving? And technically speaking, why wasn't I moving anyway if there were no forces here? Shouldn't I at least be floating?

"Maybe I shouldn't ask any more questions," I chided myself.

"Grant please focus," Niara admonished me gently. "You must use your powers of concentration. You must believe yourself to another place."

"Okay, you can do this, Granty boy!" and with that I willed myself to another position.

Nothing happened…absolutely nothing at all. I tried again with the same result. I tried again and again and again.

"What's happening, Niara? Why isn't this working? What's the trick to managing to do this?"

"Do not give up, Grant. It will take time. You must work within yourself. Once you have achieved, all things will be possible. Practise Grant and keep practising until you feel the shift," she whispered. "I will leave you now but I shall return," and with that she faded from my sight once more.

I did keep trying. I tried and tried and tried for what seemed like hours or maybe even days. I had no way of measuring time. Oh, I could work out a few minutes by counting but you can't keep that up forever.

"Sam could," I reflected.

Sam was the son of another one of my mates. He'd been born with autism so he had his problems with communication and learning, but for some reason he loved to count. He'd count anything. And what's more, he could spend hours doing it. It drove Andy, his dad, nuts sometimes. He was a great kid and the family loved him dearly.

Sam's autism fascinated me. It was such a complex disorder with so many varied facets to it. I'd come across quite a few kids on the spectrum and it amazed me how diverse the levels of disability were. They ranged from non-verbal children, with odd compulsive behaviours, to highly intelligent people with barely recognisable traits. Sometimes, the only things that would give them away were their obsessions with whatever interested them, or their inability to hold what we would deem a 'normal' conversation.

Andy told me the story of an adult with autism who was a specialist software developer. He lived, breathed and ate his job. His employer loved him. All he required was a supply of pizza and coke and he would work away happily for hours, non-stop.

One day he was called to give evidence at a court case where a company had accused the business he worked for of stealing software designs. The Queens Counsel for the opposing legal team bid him good morning before the commencement of questioning. No response. The judge asked him to respond.

"I don't know what he means," was his reply. "Is he asking me if it's a good morning or is he telling me it is a good morning?"

When it came to question time, his answers were so voluminous and detailed that in the end the lawyer threw his hands up in despair and declared,

"Enough!"

The case was thrown out of court.

My sister Keira's eldest son had Attention Deficit Hyperactivity Disorder which is also on the Autism spectrum. He was on the move from morning to night and into everything. Our mother used to say, "You need three people to look after John," and I'm sure she was right.

Not that he was a bad kid, because he wasn't, but he had no sense of danger and was as spontaneous as they come. Ever curious, he was always pulling things apart regardless of whether it was appropriate or not.

"A bit like me when I was a young 'un," I had to concede. "They were great kids, John and young Sam. I could certainly do with Sam here now. At least I'd be able to work out how long I've been attempting this."

With no day or night, there were no cycles to judge the passing of time. The only light was what glowed from me and Niara when she was around. Even then, the feebleness of our light paled into insignificance in the great pool of black nothingness which I found myself in.

The next time Niara turned up, the first question I asked her was "How much time have I wasted turning myself inside out getting nowhere?"

"You cannot waste time Grant. Time cannot be wasted ever!" Niara replied vehemently.

"Okay, okay," I conceded. "I truly need to know what time I have spent in terms I can relate to."

"As you wish Grant, but the answer may distress you and I do not want to trouble your mind."

"Niara, I'm a big boy. I can handle it," I assured her, though a seed of doubt niggled at my brain.

"At this point of time, in the method that you used to judge time, ten months on Earth has passed."

"Ten months!" I screamed.

Anger, shock, horror and amazement warred in a mass of tangled emotions.

"Ten months!"

I thought I'd had a tough time getting my head around everything which had happened so far but this was incredible. How could I have not realised ten months had passed? I would have been shocked if she'd said ten weeks! I felt as if my mind had been blown away.

It took me ages to calm down and by the time I had, Niara had left me. She knew I needed time alone to regroup my senses, and I was grateful for her absence. I was horrified to think I could possibly spend another ten months or more on this seemingly hopeless endeavour. With a sense of utter commitment, I renewed my efforts afresh.

Frustration and a little fear started to mount as I threw myself into the task of moving. The problem was, I couldn't even pinpoint a place to move to. Everywhere around me was emptiness. I concentrated as hard as I could. I even tried to meditate myself into moving. All my attempts failed abysmally.

"Try harder," I urged and continued in my quest.

Over and over and over again; relentlessly I kept on trying.

"How much more of this can I take?"

I almost felt like crying, I was so frustrated.

"Niara, help me!" I called out in anguish.

Immediately she was there.

"Grant, do not despair. You will overcome your battle," she encouraged me. "It is more difficult for you because you have never believed in what you cannot see. Those who have had faith in the things unseen find this task easier. Your mind is at war with your inner knowledge of all things. You must mend the rift within yourself so that you may move as a whole being."

I didn't know how I could possibly do that.

"Find a way to be at peace," Niara instructed, and then she was gone again.

You know, I've always thought I was at peace with myself. That's what all my studying was for. So I could be sure what I chose to believe in was in harmony with my thoughts and desires. And yet here I was being told that this was not the case. I thought of my brother, Richard and how he had to learn to be in harmony with himself.

When Richard was quite young, he started to notice he was slightly different from some of his friends. It wasn't until he reached his early teens that he realised he was gay. Our father was very homophobic and suffered mental health problems. Richard had to deal with his own issues of accepting his homosexuality, along with the certain knowledge that if our father found out, it was extremely likely that he would murder Richard before taking his own life.

Richard tried everything to become straight. He went to a psychiatrist for a number of years. He tried having a girlfriend and even had an unsuccessful attempt at sex with a prostitute. At one stage, suicide seemed to be the only alternative. He had tried to discuss it with me once, but he was being so vague I didn't have a clue what he was talking about, so I said I wasn't interested in his problems. Looking back, I can't believe what a selfish idiot I had been. Thankfully, the psychiatrist knew better and was able to convince Richard of a more appropriate alternative, which was to accept who he was. To stop fighting a war he couldn't possibly win.

Eventually, he managed to achieve that goal and had a great, successful life. He fathered two children by being a sperm donor to some lesbian friends and was fortunate enough to maintain a very close relationship with both his children. Now it was my turn to learn a different type of harmony, one I didn't even understand.

"Grant, you can't throw the towel in now," I growled. "There is a way, you've been told that, now you have to go and find it."

Once more, I threw myself into the job of moving but with renewed determination, if that was possible.

"Keep practising, keep practising, keep practising," went round and around in my head like a litany.

What passed for time spiralled ever onwards as I pushed myself along to discover the power within. I began to understand the meaning of the phrase 'When time stands still.'

"Why don't I sleep?" I'd wonder. "At least sleep would offer me some respite."

If I'd slept regularly, then I would have had some sort of indication of how long I'd been working. I felt soon I would go insane.

"That would serve Niara right for leaving me like this," I thought bitterly. "I'm sure she'd feel sorry for not helping more if she came back and found me a babbling wreck, lost in a morass of madness."

I was starting to feel very sorry for myself. Effort after effort had me despairing of ever managing to promote myself from this spot.

"I'm going to try once more with a clear mind," I murmured.

With that, I emptied every thought from my head and allowed feelings to well and grow and swell from inside. Power seemed to move from unknown parts in seething waves, whirling and churning through me.

Then suddenly it happened. I felt something shift deep within me... I moved an inch. The strain had taken what little energy was left. Drained, I blacked out.

CHAPTER V

When I awoke, I realised I'd been dreaming. Incredibly, I felt totally refreshed.

"Just goes to show what a good night's sleep can do for you," I thought wryly.

I was buzzing with excitement at achieving my hard won goal and couldn't wait for Niara to arrive so I could show off a bit. Experimenting, I found I could now move quite easily. I glided to the left, then to the right and attempted reverse.

"That one needs a bit more polish," I laughed.

Yes, I was moving quite smoothly, but I still couldn't move more than about ten feet, which was the extent of my luminary capabilities. My glow radiated in a ten foot circumference and for some reason my mind wouldn't allow me to project past that slightly comforting border.

"Fear of the unknown perhaps?" I reasoned.

I knew I'd have to overcome that eventually, but for now I was just plain ecstatic I'd made inroads. To while away the time until Niara's return and my movement debut, I began trying to recall what I had been dreaming about during my exhausted sleep.

Images floated to my consciousness and I remembered I'd dreamt about a period of my life when I'd met Laura. With a twinge of guilt, I realised I'd hardly spent any time thinking of Laura and the kids; or anyone else for that matter. I'd been so totally immersed in what I'd been trying to achieve that I hadn't given them a passing thought. Purposefully, I started re-living the past.

By this stage of my life, I'd completed my bricklaying apprenticeship and been in a subcontracting partnership for two years. I was half way through my Clerk of Works course, attending a TAFE college three nights a week. I had plenty of work and the money was good.

I was always an excellent saver and poured every spare cent into my share of the house I'd bought with Richard. By the time I'd turned twenty-two I'd paid off my half and then the wanderlust hit. I tossed my partnership in to travel around the country with Steve.

"Strange how my mind keeps going back to Steve," I pondered.

He'd lived with his family a few doors up from us in a small cul-de-sac. It had taken a while before Steve told me that Richard and I had been the subject of many laughs for him and his brothers.

You see, they were the outdoors, adventurous types and a bundle of male testosterone their mother and father didn't try too hard to contain. We, on the other hand, had a very protective mother who worried herself sick over any situation which might bring us harm. I didn't get a pushbike until I was nearly twelve and even then I was only allowed to ride it around the circle of the cul-de-sac.

Around and around my brother and I would ride, looking like goldfish in a bowl, much to the bemusement of the Andrew's family. I had to laugh thinking back on how I'd thought he was nuts for running around in circles on the oval.

My laughter started me thinking about Steve's laughter. For some reason I could get him to laugh harder and more often than anyone else. Tears would roll down his face and he'd bend over, stomping a foot on the ground, gasping for breath. All it would take would be for me to do something simple, like imitate my grandfather.

"The music has started again," I suddenly realised. "It must be time for my mental massage. Ah, that feels so good," I thought as I wallowed in the pure beauty of it.

So intense was the pleasure, it was an effort to resume my reminiscing. I had to push myself to make my becalmed mind work.

"Now where was I?"

My grandfather had landed in the middle of my family when I was about sixteen and he'd rubbed me up the wrong way from the start. I guess it was hard on all of us. The problem was that he didn't know us and we didn't know him. We'd never been able to form a connection in those vital younger years.

He'd lived in England after the split with our grandmother and eventually remarried. Keeping in touch with our mother via letters was fine for her, but he was an unknown entity to the rest of us. When his second wife died,

Mum invited him to live with us in our small, cold government-owned house.

To put a stranger in a house with three teenage children and a daughter you hadn't seen for twenty years was just asking for trouble. We couldn't escape each other and my Grandfather, being in his seventies, was pretty set in his ways. It wasn't long before everything he said and did started to annoy us and I vented by mimicking him behind his back.

One day he'd accompanied us to where we kept our horses. It had been raining and there was mud and puddles everywhere. The only way around one particularly large section of mud and water was to climb onto the post and rail fence and sidle along. Not to be outdone, the old boy decided he was still agile enough to do the same as the rest of us.

He managed to clamber onto the rails and began the trip around the muddy water. Apparently pleased with his efforts, he began calling out to our mother,

"Margaret, Margaret, look at me!"

So anxious was he to gain her attention, he must have forgotten to hold on tight, for the next minute he was flat on his back right in the middle of the mud pool. The sight of him floundering like an upside down turtle was a sight to behold. His portly stomach jutted into the air while his short arms and legs flapped around helplessly. It took some effort to haul him out of the muddy mess. Steve loved that story. I'd only have to say,

"Margaret, Margaret, look at me!" in my rendition of the old boy's voice and Steve would be off.

Of course the more he laughed, the more I kept it up, until I'd have him in absolute agony. Steve suffered from asthma and there were times he would be laughing so hard he couldn't catch his breath. He would beg me sometimes in between gasps,

"Grant shut up, please just shut up!"

Of course I wouldn't. It was just too hilarious watching him laugh even if he couldn't breathe at the time. I had lots of ammunition up my sleeve to get him going and I used them all.

It's weird to think I don't breathe anymore. It gets my head undone if I dwell on it too long. I guess that's what Niara was trying to get through to me in the first place when she said, 'You just are…'

"C'mon Granty, you need to think about something else, old son, before you go crazy."

We were both pretty happy when we set off on our trip. Steve and I had planned to travel north, up the New South Wales and Queensland coastline as far as Cairns. Steve loved the ocean. He was never quite as happy as when he was near the water. His parents owned a holiday home on the South Coast and the family would go down there every weekend. That's what probably engendered his love of anything to do with the sea.

Steve was fearless in the water and after surfing; his next biggest love was spear fishing. Around the South Coast were small sharks called Wobbegongs which averaged about six feet in length and were harmless, although they had razor sharp teeth. Steve would dive down, reach under a ledge and grab one of them by the tail and try to drag it out so his brothers could get a spear into it. The shark would twist around, lunging at Steve, trying to bite him in its frantic efforts to be free. After a struggle, the boys would eventually get their spears into the shark and then Steve could spear it as well.

Once, all the brother's spears were shaken free, leaving Steve alone with this six foot shark. Single-handed he managed to tire the shark out and drag it to shore with an amazing feat of strength and endurance.

Another shark encounter was with a nine foot grey nurse. These sharks aren't normally aggressive but are big enough to seriously hurt somebody under extreme circumstances. I'd just gotten out of the water and was resting on the rocks when Steve came across the shark. He herded it into a shallow, natural rock pool and kept swimming just above it, all the while calling me to come back in to play with the shark. I called back in what I hoped sounded like a laconic reply,

"I'm pretty comfortable right where I am, thanks all the same."

After about fifteen minutes of Steve annoying this shark, it had obviously decided enough was enough. Breaking the surface of the water with its dorsal fins, it started circling Steve. Steve laughingly relented and sang out to me,

"I suppose I'd better let her go. She's starting to get a bit agro."

With that he swam to the side of the rock pool and the shark took off into the safety of deep water.

"Deep water eh?" I questioned myself as I started trying to project myself past the safety of my own light with steely determination, jumping into the deep end if you like.

With each failed attempt my resolve crumbled a bit.

"I will keep on trying but I'm positive I'm way out of my depth," I groaned.

Thinking so much about deep water reminded me of another spear fishing expedition when Steve, three of his brothers and I, borrowed Steve's father's twelve foot 'tinnie.' The twelve foot aluminium boat didn't have a motor at the time, so we took turns rowing the forty minutes to be near an island they knew of. Once there, we jumped into the water looking for fish to spear.

Unfortunately for me, I swam into a large swarm of Bluebottle jellyfish. Bluebottles are quite small; their bodies are generally only two to four inches long. When they get washed ashore their bodies fill up with air and they resemble little blue bottles which pop if you step on them. Though their bodies are small, they have one very long tentacle which can stretch out for a number of feet.

This particular day I swam into hundreds of them. I had tentacles across my face, around my throat, over my chest, back, arms and legs. Each sting was equivalent to the agony of a wasp sting and I had a lot of stings. To realise how toxic they are, one sting can paralyse a medium size fish. By the time I returned to the boat I was in agony, although I did my best not to show it.

I had always been the same about showing pain. I don't know if it was because my mother thought it was a sign of weakness if men expressed much emotion, or whether it was some primordial instinct which said a predator would get you if you showed you were sick or injured. Either way, I always tried to put on a brave face.

Once inside the boat, Steve and his brothers pulled off all the tentacles before administering their own peculiar brand of first aid. Their first instruction was for me to stay in the boat until they had finished spear fishing. After waiting forty-five minutes for the boys to catch their quota and everyone was back on board, they issued their second first aid instruction. I was to do all the rowing on the return journey, as this would take my mind off the pain.

Whilst I have never seen any of this written in any type of medical journal and common sense tells me it was a pretty risky form of treatment, I must admit it did appear to work, particularly in my arms. By the time I had rowed the full forty minutes, my arms were like lead and I couldn't feel a thing. I counted myself lucky there weren't too many times I was left to their tender mercies.

Wearily, I realised the wondrous music seemed to be playing more often now. Thinking about it, I decided it was pretty obvious, with all my attempts at shifting, I must be exhausting myself. Logically, the solution would be to rest more often. And while I was resting, it would be a good opportunity to reflect on events in my past. I still hadn't discovered where I went wrong with my belief system and it was a rankling annoyance which needed to be resolved.

"I'm convinced I need to work it all out before I'm able to move on and the only way I'm going to do that is to keep sifting through my memories," I asserted with more conviction than I actually felt.

When we left Canberra to start our year long trip up north, Steve was determined to teach me how to surf. Being a no-nonsense type of guy, he wasn't going to make it easy. His strategy was to throw the student into the deep end first. No gentle two foot swells for me. No, it had to be four feet or above, preferably way above. Every time we went into the surf I would be smashed by the waves and it would take forty-five minutes just to get through the breakers. By the time I'd struggled through, turned around and tried to catch a wave, I would be too exhausted to go through the whole process again.

It reminded me of the first time I went snow skiing with him. My brother Richard, my cousin Kate and I had never skied before. Steve, who had been skiing for about six years, went through the rudiments, explaining how to do the snow plough, turns and stopping. After thirty minutes of lessons he decided it was time to put what he'd taught us into practice.

He put us on a chairlift to the biggest, steepest mountain he could find and then left us to find our own way back down. We spent far more time on our backsides than on our skis. My poor cousin became so exhausted that eventually she found it nearly impossible to stand up. It must have been hilarious for anyone watching the spectacle of Kate lying in the snow with Richard and I sliding all over the place in our efforts to help her to her feet, only for us to end up falling over each other or on top of Kate. What a debacle.

It took so long to get down the mountain that it started to get dark. Thankfully, the ski patrol showed up to clear the slopes. They were able to get on either side of Kate and ski her down the rest of the mountain while Richard and I skied and tumbled at a fast enough rate to keep up with the patrolmen. When we got back down and told Steve of our adventure, he laughed so hard he had tears in his eyes. He was disappointed he hadn't hung around to watch us. Over the years I did become a reasonable skier but I never did learn how to surf on that trip up north with Steve.

"I wonder if I should call Niara and show her what I still can't do?" I thought forlornly, my inability to move beyond the light never far from my mind.

"No, I don't want to be a nuisance; I'll wait a little longer. I'm sure she'll be here soon enough."

I settled back into my thoughts, determined to be patient.

It was during our northern adventure that I first set eyes on Laura. Steve and I had gone our separate ways when we reached Cairns. Steve's priority was to earn some big money on the trawlers while I'd already been used to having a very good income in Canberra with my work as a bricklaying contractor. I was more interested in the travelling experience and trying anything which didn't involve masonry.

After working on a dairy farm on the Atherton Tablelands for a couple of months and then doing a stint in Innisfail working on renovating concrete trucks, I changed plans and headed west to the Northern Territory. On the way, I stopped for a few days in Mount Isa, a lead, zinc, copper and silver mining city in the far west of Queensland.

It was rodeo time there, so I decided to go to the local dance which was being held at the Overlander Hotel to meet some of the girls. I spotted Laura in the first thirty minutes. I admired her shoulder length blonde hair and big blue eyes. At five feet three inches tall and weighing around one hundred and ten pounds, I found her body very appealing. She was the only one to hold any interest for me so I watched her for awhile.

She was busy rejecting all the local boys that were coming over and asking for a dance. North Queenslanders have a peculiar habit of adding "ay" to the end of every sentence.

"You wanna dance, ay?"

"No thanks," Laura would reply.

"Got into a fight last week, ay."

"Really," said Laura.

"Yeah, broke me arm, ay," said the guy, showing her the cast on his arm. "Yeah, but the other guy got a lot worse, ay. Sure ya don't wanna dance, ay?"

"Yes, I'm quite sure," Laura reasserted.

He'd wander off, only to be replaced a few minutes later by someone else asking her for a dance with the obligatory "ay" on the end of the request. After taking this spectacle in, I decided she wasn't a local and I'd be better off not asking for a dance. I sat down beside her and asked where she was from and where she was heading. I think she was relieved I wasn't using the North Queensland vernacular and proceeded to tell me,

"I'm travelling with my brother, his fiancé and their child, along with two dogs, in a blue van. My sister, Robbie, decided to join us at the last minute along with a family friend, Mario and they are travelling with me in my little Datsun 180B to Darwin."

I did eventually get one dance out of her that night but that's as far as it went. I didn't think I'd ever see her again. They started their thousand mile journey to Darwin the next morning while I decided to hang around Mt Isa a few more days. I reached Darwin a couple of weeks later and pulled in to the largest caravan park there at the time, The Shady Glen.

I'd been thinking about Laura off and on over the last two weeks, so I decided to walk around the entire camp ground on the off-chance they had decided to stay there also. I'd just about given up when I came across a blue van with two dogs tied to it, right at the far end of the campground.

"This could be the van she was talking about," I postulated.

I'd just finished the thought and turned to head back to my campsite when there she was, driving up the road in her trusty little 180B…

Suddenly Niara materialised, snapping me out of my reveries.

"Look Niara, look! I can do it!" and I glided towards her.

"I knew you had accomplished your task. I felt the shift," she exclaimed. "Well done. Now you must grow in power so that you may move further."

"Is that going to take as long as the last task?" I asked her warily.

"I do not believe so," she said reassuringly. "I feel that you have passed the biggest hurdle in this transition and the rest will be easier for you."

Uneasily I wondered what else I might be in for and decided not to explore the question further for the moment. I was quite happy not to have anything else to worry about for the next little while. Instead, I decided to ask Niara about some of the other things which had been intriguing me.

"How can I see without eyes and hear without ears?"

"I am surprised you are asking these questions Grant. You had an out of body experience at your death, did you not? Were you not able to see and hear everything?"

"Yes," I responded. "But I wasn't completely dead. My heart had stopped but my brain was still alive," I asserted.

"That is true Grant, though your eyes were closed and yet you could still see from above. An entirely different perspective from where your body actually was. Besides this, your mind is still active is it not, even without a brain?"

She had me there.

"Yes, I guess it is," I answered.

"We are able to communicate telepathically. We are simply picking up each other's thoughts, much like a radar signal. There is no need for a mouth or tongue," Niara continued.

"I've heard of people claiming to be able to do one or both of these things and they didn't need to become like this to achieve it," I challenged her.

"That is correct Grant. They have managed to tap the power within."

"What is this power within?" I enquired, feeling as if I was on the edge of a momentous discovery.

Niara didn't disappoint me.

"Why, it is the life force... the essence of existence and more powerful than you can ever imagine. Some have called it the 'soul' but it is more than an individual's entity. It is part of the Creator. That is how you are able to leave the mortal body and still see, hear, communicate and retain every word, thought or experience you have ever had."

I had the feeling that I was getting in a bit over my head but I decided to persevere.

"How are we able to communicate with others who have died and spoken a different language in their past lives?"

"Grant, we mainly think in images. Our thoughts become universal here," she related. "You will be able to communicate with everyone once the opportunity arises. For now though, you must continue to acquire the knowledge of movement and learn how to move that twinkling little behind of yours more than ten feet!"

"Niara," I burst out. "You actually have a sense of humour," and we both laughed. "Just one more question, please."

"Your request is granted," she teased.

"Is there anything which this life force thing can't do?"

"The power within and without enables you to move mountains and more if that is what you wish."

"That sounds as if you're talking about miracles and surely there's no substance to miracles, is there?"

"Miracles are events which appear inexplicable by the laws of nature," Niara explained. "Scientists do not believe in miracles as they cannot be explained by those very laws. Mobile phones and computers would have been considered miracles two hundred years prior to their invention. Just because you do not have the knowledge, does not make a miracle impossible. The Creator has the knowledge to expand with the laws of nature so that while they may appear miraculous to others, they are easily explained and understood by the Creator. And Grant, that was two questions!" she said accusingly and with that she was gone.

CHAPTER VI

Niara had given me a lot to think about. When I was alive, I would sometimes get a believer to describe what their version of Heaven would be like. Different people would come up with all sorts of wonderful visions incorporating their hearts desires. And you know what? To me it all sounded really boring!

After I'd analysed why I felt that way, it boiled down to the old adage 'Too much of a good thing.' The problem with the idea of Heaven, to my way of thinking, was how do you occupy yourself forever and ever and ever? Life on Earth could be exciting because you didn't live long enough to experience everything the planet had to offer.

For me personally, I usually received far more pleasure pursuing a goal than actually achieving it. I knew a number of people who'd spent years striving to reach their targets only to become utterly depressed once they'd managed to get there. I mean, what reason was left for them to get up in the morning? They'd lost the fire in their bellies, their raison d'etre and the thing which drove them to keep going. They only became happy again once they'd found a new goal to spark their interest.

Was I in Heaven? If so, it wasn't like anything I'd ever read about or envisaged. There certainly weren't any fluffy white clouds or winged angels with harps flying around that I'd come across. No Saint Peter at the pearly gates either. Niara had simply called this place the Afterlife. I made a mental note to ask her if this was what humankind called Heaven?

If this was Heaven and I could describe it to someone, I'd have to say it couldn't sound more dreary, depressing and utterly boring. You don't eat, you don't drink, there is no-one to talk to ninety-five percent of the time and there is absolutely nothing to see and I mean nothing. No sun, wind, rain, mountains or streams. Not even a crummy rock. It's a completely black, empty vacuum of space. To top it all off, I spend virtually all of my time just trying to teach myself to move a few feet and it's mentally exhausting. I had imagined Heaven boring but never hard.

I'm sure if I could tell my mates about it they'd say, "Sorry Grant, but I think you took a left turn at Albuquerque and ended up in the other place where all good atheists go."

However, as bad as all that sounds, amazingly it isn't. In fact, I'm having an incredible experience. I think it must be because I can't gauge myself against anything. Not time, performance or past experience. There is absolutely no pressure. I know it sounds weird but it feels liberating and cathartic. At the moment, I am freer and more at peace than I ever was when I was alive. I wonder if people who meditate for years at a time, sometimes in complete isolation, feel like this.

I'm also able to focus for seemingly endless periods. I'd never tried marijuana when I was alive but I'd had friends who had. They told me of their experiences whilst high, of staring at one object for hours and loving every second of it. Maybe this is something like that? Or maybe my image of time is so distorted that I can't differentiate between seconds, minutes, hours, days, weeks or even years. It doesn't really seem to matter. This feeling of blissfulness is very addictive.

Dramatic as ever, I realise Niara is back to check up on me. The first question I ask is,

"How come I feel so content? Have I achieved inner peace?"

"No Grant, you have a long journey ahead to achieve inner peace. It is the Creator's presence and energy which is greater here than on Earth. It is this energy that is providing you with feelings of euphoria."

I stopped and thought about that for a while before I pounced with question two.

"Who or what is the Creator and does it have a name?" I asked.

Suddenly, this question became of paramount importance to me. I really needed to know.

"How ironic," I caught myself thinking. "Me needing to know about a Creator, something I'd rubbished my whole life."

I felt rather subdued while I waited for her answer.

"We call the Creator Nyame and it is the most powerful, conscious energy in the Universe," she exclaimed. "Nyame's existence coincided exactly with the beginnings of the Universe... Nyame is found in everything. In fact, Nyame and the Universe are inextricably linked."

"How does that work?" I asked credulously.

"Do you understand that space and time are inextricably linked?" Niara questioned.

"Yes, to a certain extent."

"So you understand, if you bend space through strong gravitational forces, you bend time also, because time is a dimension, just like width, height and length. Black holes are an example of how this works. Space in a black hole is distorted to a great degree because of the massive gravitational forces working on it," she lectured.

"If you think of a river reaching a waterfall, you would notice the current increasing its pace the closer it gets to the edge. Space reacts in exactly the same way, leading up to and going over the edge of a black hole. Stephen Hawkins, a cosmologist of your era, explained it like this so you may better understand," Niara continued.

"Imagine a spaceship orbiting a super-massive black hole at the centre of the Milky Way galaxy twenty-six thousand light years away from Earth. From an observer on Earth's perspective, it would appear the ship was making an orbit every sixteen minutes. For the intrepid voyagers within the ship however, time would be slowed down close to the massive object.

"For every sixteen minute orbit they would only experience eight minutes of time. If they circled the black hole for five years local time, ten years would have passed back on Earth. This shows that space and time are linked and they can be bent. However, there is much more to it.

"Space and time are actually part of a trilogy. Nyame is the third part of space and time and they cannot be separated. They are completely interwoven; as the Universe expands, so does Nyame.

"Your cosmologists are trying to come up with a unified theory so they have a law which explains how everything in the Universe works. One of the problems they have encountered is there appears to be more mass in the Universe than what they can account for. Part of that unaccountable additional mass is Nyame. When you say that God is omnipresent, you have no idea how literally true that is," she declared.

I tried to let these facts burrow deep inside before I made a comment but I just couldn't help myself.

"Wow!" was all I could think to say. "Nyame is a super conscious energy which is interwoven with space and time and pervades every nook and cranny of the entire Universe. That is big! That is mind boggling big!

"I feel so stupid. All those years of being totally convinced there was no possibility of a supernatural consciousness which some humans called God. I never believed this could possibly exist and yet there it is in everything I have ever seen or touched my entire life. It was there all along. Talk about being blind. How could I have not felt it, or him, or is it a her?" I wondered.

"Niara, is Nyame a male or a female?"

"Grant, that is like asking whether the Universe is male or female. Nyame is sexless. Nyame does not have an original form. Nyame is vigorous in power," she told me. "As for why you could not feel the presence of

Nyame, you chose not to. You were led astray as so many on Earth have been and continue to be."

"What do you mean, led astray?"

Niara explained, "You have a scripture that says, 'It is easier for a rich man to pass through the eye of a needle than to enter the gates of Heaven.' You could interpret that message this way. A wealthy person is usually too distracted by the pursuit of material riches to feel the presence of Nyame. The joy the affluent person feels in the pursuit of his treasure is nothing compared to the joy he could experience in Nyame's presence.

"You have experienced that exquisite pleasure since your arrival. I can feel you had many possessions while you were still alive Grant. Did they actually bring you delight? Your time on Earth was shared with people too busy either surviving or chasing targets to truly enjoy life, to stop and feel."

This is amazing. How many times could I get it wrong? Niara was spot on. I did have a lot of possessions. A big house, two or three cars, multiple televisions, the list went on and on. I even had two large dining room suites. Why, I don't know, especially since there was just the two of us most of the time. And it hadn't made me happy. Sure it was good to show off to my friends, a way of proving that I was relatively successful, but deep down I felt my life was full of clutter. So much so that sometimes I felt I was drowning in it.

Thinking back, some of the happiest times of my life were when we were the poorest. Mum and Dad had split up when I was twelve and money was tighter than ever before. Not that there had ever been much money when Dad was around. By the time he'd had his beers, gambled on the horses, played Bingo and put a fair whack down the poker machines, there wasn't a great deal left for the household expenses.

Mum and Dad's marriage had been tumultuous to say the least and their fights had impacted on Keira, Richard and I, profoundly at times. Even now I can remember the feelings of anxiety which would well when an argument was brewing. Too often, those arguments would end with our father's fist in our mother's face. It never stopped Mum from putting herself in a position to be hit again the next time she perceived injustice from him, something we kids could never understand. We would beg her to keep quiet and not to nag him, all to no avail.

Our father liked things his way and his way meant that he could do whatever he wanted, whenever he wanted. If there was anything left over after that, then he could magnanimously allow us to take the crumbs. Mum always blamed his mother for his attitude. Our grandmother thought the sun, moon and stars shone from her two sons.

She'd been a single mum from the time she came home from the hospital with her second child, Dad's brother. Perhaps to make up for not having a father in those days when divorce was rare, she'd pampered the boys to the extreme. Both of them were very good looking and the women flocked to them in droves. It was other women that impacted on our parents' marriage.

I can remember Mum telling us on more than one occasion of a time when Dad had a headache just before they were married. His mother had wrapped the light bulbs in brown paper so that the glare wouldn't cause him any further pain. Mum was disgusted at her mother-in-law's over-the-top solicitousness toward her adult son.

A few years later, when Keira had broken her arm as a baby and Dad wouldn't take her to a doctor because he thought it was a sprain, his mother's thoughts had immediately flown to how her son must feel when Mum came home from the hospital with Keira's arm in plaster.

"Poor Brian!" was all his mother could say. "He must feel so dreadful about this. Don't make him feel any worse," was her advice to her daughter-in-law.

She felt sorry for her son, despite the fact she knew Mum had endured Dad's abuse for insisting on seeing a doctor. Mum had a long train ride to the hospital because Dad refused to take her and then suffered interrogation and suspicion from hospital staff, who couldn't understand why she had waited so long to obtain treatment for a fracture.

Unfortunately for everyone concerned, including my father, his parent created a selfish person who believed the world revolved around his desires. I'm sure he loved his family in his own way but his own wants drowned out the needs of everybody else. His own mother became the victim of both her son's hedonistic ways. They loved her but they got on with their own lives, leaving a woman bereft and useless. She had devoted every minute of every day to her children and without them she had no purpose in life. Her sixty-third birthday arrived without a card or phone call from either of her sons, so she turned the gas on and killed herself.

It was the first and only time I ever saw my father cry. Two telegrams had arrived in the afternoon from the police informing us of his mother's death. When we told him Nana had died he asked,

"Which Nana?"

When we broke the news that it was his mother, his reaction was muted. In hindsight I can see that shock played a big part in his apparent unconcernedness. It was only as we sat together for the evening meal that the realisation of his mother's untimely demise must have hit him. Silent tears rolled down his face and onto his unfinished meal.

He blew his inheritance on having a good time. He'd met a woman prior to this, but it was months later before Mum had absolute proof. She'd always suspected his infidelities but without concrete evidence she didn't really have a leg to stand on. I think he just got careless in the end. Only the evening before her discovery, Dad had come to Mum and said,

"I may have a funny way of showing it but I do love you."

The very next evening, Mum found him in a car with his mistress, a woman who had been told by our Dad that Mum was his sister. By the time she found out Mum was his wife, she had fallen in love. This woman had nine children from a previous relationship. If she'd only known she'd gone from the pot to the frying pan.

After the confrontation at the car, Mum walked home and was joined shortly after by Dad.

"What's for dinner?" was the first thing he asked.

Mum threw his dinner at him.

"Marg, Marg, don't be upset," he consoled her. "Lots of men do this. It doesn't mean anything."

He didn't seem to get it that it meant everything to his wife.

The day Mum demanded he leave the house was one of the happiest days of my life. I could see he didn't want to go and had hoped that, given enough time, Mum would cool down and let him have his cake and eat it too. He should have known better. Mum was a terrier at the best of times but now she absolutely rose to the occasion.

The first thing she did was play an LP record entitled 'Please Release Me' at full bore for the next twenty-four hours. To this day I cannot bear that song. She threw his clothes out the windows into the front yard. Holes were pricked into his condoms and joined the clothes. The tirade of her abuse was incessant. The neighbours walked backward and forward having a lovely time.

Dad's car had developed mechanical problems that very day and he'd called a serviceman to come to the house. I'd love to have known what the repairman was thinking as he worked on the car. He never once lifted his head from the motor despite all the objects which were streaming from the interior of the house and my mother's constant harangue of invective. I can only imagine it was a story he'd tell for many years to come. Anyway, I didn't want to dwell on that subject anymore. The happy times came after he left.

It was during this period that Richard and I collected our animals and grew our hair longer, as was the fashion of the day, something our father would never have allowed if he'd been at home. Keira left school to help make ends meet and life settled into a positively peaceful and happy time. We spent evening's together playing cards, we had friends come over and the intimidation which had ruled our lives ceased.

It must have been difficult in many ways for Mum but she never complained. She worked full time at a fruit and vegetable shop, then came home and cooked the meals, washed, ironed, sewed and cleaned. How she did it I'll never know because we certainly didn't help her. Oh, we did a few odd things. Richard and I would chop wood and every now and again Keira would help clean the house, but the bulk of the work fell on Mum's shoulders and we didn't give it a thought. It's so easy to take what is freely given.

Things changed a few years later when Richard and I bought our first house but until then Mum had her work cut out for her. Having said that, Mum was as happy as the rest of us, not having Dad around. It was like a great weight had been lifted from the family. In many respects we got on better with Dad once he wasn't living with us. Mind you, we felt deeply sorry for his new family. We all got on fine, Mum included, with Doris and her kids. In the end, Mum would accompany Doris to play Bingo and would be a shoulder to cry on when Doris was having problems with Dad.

Yes, we were dirt poor in those years but I look back on that time very fondly. We always had plenty to eat, even if we didn't have more than a couple of sets of clothes to choose from or any of the so-called mod cons. We had the necessities of life rather than the luxuries, but when it comes down to it, that's all we require, isn't it? Why then, did I pursue the course of materialism?

Previously, I'd always argued you couldn't be truly happy in life without having a goal to strive for. Now, through Niara, I've discovered it's the exact opposite. You can't experience true happiness with too many distractions in life or you won't be able to feel Nyame's presence.

"Will I ever get this right?" I wondered. "And did Niara mean all goals are bad or was she just talking about financial goals?"

Realising that Niara was still before me, I felt compelled to ask, "Niara are all goals bad?"

"Grant, it is not a case of whether goals are good or bad; it is whether they are distracting or not. Many goals are benevolent and can be very helpful in your journey. Even financial goals can give you security to allow you to have the time to feel, or the ability to help others who are just too busy surviving. The quest for true inner peace is very difficult to achieve. The first step is to let go, unclog your mind and feel."

"Easier said than done when you're wondering where the next meal or the next deal is coming from," I thought grimly to myself.

But then I started to wonder if animals might have had a better chance of experiencing inner peace than humans? After all, they don't have anywhere near the problems that Homo sapiens seem to be able to inflict on themselves.

"What about animals, Niara? Are there any animals in this place?"

"No Grant," she replied. "Only the chosen ones are here; humans from Earth."

"Why not animals?"

"Because that is the way it is and that is all you need to know for now," she responded firmly.

I could tell Niara was getting a bit irritated with my line of questioning but I pressed on anyway.

"When will I get to speak to Nyame?"

Unflustered, Niara responded with, "Never Grant. No-one speaks to Nyame, not even us."

I was confused.

"How does that work?"

"When Nyame requires us to perform a task, we feel the request and then we perform it unquestioningly. You Grant, are a long way off from feeling a request or doing anything without a question!" she retorted.

Not to be outdone I responded, "You said that Nyame doesn't talk to you, yet this Creator has an African name. How did you learn the name?"

"The name was chosen by more ancient Beings. The Creator didn't give them the feeling of rejection so the name has remained."

I decided to change tack and ask her another question.

"Can Nyame take on a human form?"

Hesitantly she answered, "In a way, Nyame does all the time."

Before I could ask what she meant, Niara continued with,

"I think that is enough questions for now. We will talk further at another time. You need to quieten your mind and keep working on moving more than a few feet."

Without further ado my taskmistress left me again.

"Where does sanity stop and madness kick in? I'd better hope I'm around for eternity, because it's going to take that long to get my head around all of this... Oh well, I guess if I'm going to avoid Niara's wrath, I'd better take her advice and get back to work," I mused.

CHAPTER VII

It didn't feel as if a great deal of time had passed until I was once more joined by Niara. I hadn't properly digested our last meeting but I was ever anxious to have the different questions answered which popped into my mind. First though, I was going to apologise for my endless questioning. I knew how I'd feel if someone kept badgering me for answers every time I came into contact with them.

"Niara, I'm sorry for inundating you with questions every time I see you, but I keep thinking things over and find I require answers to give me some respite from the thoughts which keep torturing me."

"Grant," she said gently, "I understand. It is imperative you contemplate your former existence. Unless you do, you will never learn to problem-solve."

"Problem-solve. Me? She must have the wrong person," was all I could think. "I've spent my life solving problems. I'm a master at it."

My mind immediately flew to the time Laura and I had decided to embark on an overseas trip before we married. Everything that could go wrong had gone wrong and I'd managed to find a way through thick and thin.

"Niara, please let me tell you a story about a time I was inundated with problems. I'm sure you'll change your mind once I'm finished."

"Very well, this should be interesting. I love a good story."

"Laura and I arrived in Auckland, New Zealand after a three hour flight. The wet weather arrival didn't worry me as it was summer. The clouds from the 'Land Of The Long White Cloud' weren't going to stick around for long at this time of the year. Little did I realise how wrong I could be. Back in those days, not many people used bank credit cards in Australia. American Express seemed to be the most popular card at the time so I opted for that. However, it didn't take long before I discovered the situation was even worse in New Zealand and the majority of businesses wouldn't even accept the Amex card. The bank I used in Australia wasn't available in New Zealand and had no affiliation branches either. I'd brought the maximum amount of cash allowable which was $2,600 and automatic teller machines didn't exist.

"Out of the money I'd brought in, I had to buy a car and survive for the next two months. Laura had brought her own money which amounted to around $1,000. We found an old car after a couple of days, a 1963 Ford Cortina station wagon which had been around the block quite a number of times. Two hundred and fifty-five thousand miles around the block to be exact! That's quite a lot of miles for a small, four cylinder car.

"However, I knew I was pretty handy with vehicle repairs, so I decided the car didn't need to be brilliant. We were planning just to dawdle along and check out the sights. After all, New Zealand is a relatively small country. What could go wrong?

"In Australia, the going price for a car of that vintage and mileage would have been no more than $200. Here, I went through my first steep learning curve. Anything made out of steel was going to be many times dearer than it would be back home. The asking price was $1,000. After some tense negotiating, I managed to acquire our transport for the bargain price of $800.

"I was so pleased with my bargaining skills that I failed to take proper notice of the look of trepidation that crossed the former owner's face when I explained we were planning on circumnavigating both islands. His quiet words of advice, that I should 'take it very slowly,' failed to set off alarm bells. Possibly the pelting rain distracted me!

"The short three hour drive to Rotorua was uneventful, apart from one of the headlights calling it quits and the bottom radiator hose splitting. Fortunately, I was able to replace the hose before we ran out of water. We stayed in Rotorua a few days, marvelling at the numerous mud pools, hot springs and geysers, all viewed from beneath the protection of our umbrella. The rain that we had expected would only last a day seemed to be determined to hang around a little longer. The locals assured us the rain wouldn't last much longer, being summer and all.

"Gisborne was reached by a winding road; steep in some sections but with magnificent views over the valleys. I was driving at an average speed of only thirty-five miles per hour but it seemed to take its toll on the little Cortina. By the time I'd completed the one hundred and eighty mile journey, the other headlight had gone along with the top radiator hose and unbelievably, the universal joint in the tail shaft had collapsed, making the car vibrate so badly I could barely hang onto the steering wheel.

"After a few days in Gisborne, all the repairs were done. We had added curtains to the back for privacy, a mattress for comfort and purchased a camping stove and gas bottle to save money by cooking our own food. Things were looking good. It had even stopped raining. Sure, the rain had been replaced with a thick blanket of cloud and a light drizzle, but that was much easier to cope with while working on the car and we were able to replace the umbrella with raincoats which made sightseeing simpler.

"I was happy and confident that everything was now under control and we left Gisborne to continue our journey. That is, we tried to leave Gisborne. We hadn't made it out of town before the muffler fell off. I didn't want to waste too much time or money, so I patched it up as best I could with wire and muffler bandage. We were back on the road within an hour.

"The one hundred and thirty-three miles to Napier took a little longer than expected. Again, the road was very undulating, winding in and out of the valleys with breathtaking views of both the coast and the hinterland. In some sections the mountainsides were so precipitous that if you drove off the edge you wouldn't hit the side until you reached the bottom a thousand feet below. The latter stages of the journey were further delayed by my inability to get the car out of first gear. No matter how hard I pushed or pulled, the gearstick was stuck fast. We just made it into town before the car overheated.

"Trying to make the best of it, we decided to have lunch and wait for the car to cool down before driving around to look for a mechanic. With food in our stomachs and an air of determination, we commenced our search. We couldn't help noticing how exceedingly friendly the locals were, as so many of them were waving at us… albeit with clenched fists. We weren't sure whether this was a Kiwi custom or had something to do with the fact that the top speed of our vehicle was now fifteen miles per hour and we had a trail of cars behind us."

"You were meaning that to be amusing were you not Grant?"

"Yes Niara, I was being facetious."

"Interesting; please continue."

"Finally, we found a mechanic who took one look and delivered the bad news. The gearbox was irreparable. At the time it did cross my mind that the odds of any car having this many problems in such a short period must be astronomical. Surely after this repair there couldn't be any more breakdowns? The rain started again in earnest. Uneasily, I wondered if the rain was a sign of things to come. I opted for a new gearbox for $220 rather than risk putting in a second-hand one from the wreckers. It was more money than I wanted to spend but I figured it would be one less problem to worry about.

"It was pretty easy driving the one hundred and seventy miles down the coast to Wellington; although the incessant rain had finally managed to penetrate the spark plug leads which was causing the car to cough and splutter. A quick replacement of both leads and spark plugs and I had the car purring like a kitten in no time. As far as capital cities go Niara, you should see Wellington, it was stunning.

"Situated on a picturesque harbour and dwarfed by the mountains surrounding it, Wellington seemed to be too pretty to be the capital of a country. After spending a few days there, we were ready to tackle the much larger South Island. The rain had eased back to just a light drizzle so we were feeling upbeat about the second stage of our journey.

"The first little hiccup occurred when we discovered that the ferry service which was going to deliver us and the car over the Cook Straight to the South Island didn't accept American Express as payment. I understood credit card use was still in its infancy in Australasia but this was a major New Zealand ferry line with a monopoly on the Straight. Tourists came from all over the world needing to use this mode of transport to cross from one island to the other. Crazy as it was, it made no difference. If we wanted to get to Picton, I was going to have to part with more of my dwindling cash reserves.

"Once on board, the trip was great. We had the pleasure of meeting a lovely lady, Kaye, who was travelling with her ten year old son, Brad. Most of the trip was spent competing against Brad playing video games. You've probably never heard of video games have you Niara?"

"I am aware of their existence Grant."

"Oh okay. Well Kaye was kind enough to offer us a place to stay when we had completed our trip and made it back to Auckland. We didn't realise at the time what a godsend that would be.

"After disembarking and saying our farewells, we left Picton for Christchurch. Miracle of miracles, we completed the entire two hundred and ten mile journey without a single breakdown. Things were looking up. The only slight negative about looking up though was the weather had taken a turn for the worse. The light drizzle had become heavy rain once more. I was beginning to believe 'the long white cloud' New Zealand is famous for was like a rainbow. You could never get to the end of it no matter how hard you tried.

"Christchurch was beautiful, a real university city. It was the first place I had ever been where some people actually carry a soapbox around with them, plonk it on the ground, climb on top and start spruiking about whatever it was that was important to them. It was a tragedy to see this glorious city in ruins many years later when, in 2011, an earthquake struck destroying numerous buildings in the city centre and taking the lives of one hundred and eighty people."

"Unfortunately, nature does not make allowances for areas where people choose to live," Niara stated as a matter of fact. "What happened next?"

"It was Christmas day when we decided to leave Christchurch. The rain had eased back to the customary drizzle and we thought it would be nice to drive on the roads with virtually no traffic. At the time, I was convinced there must have been at least one god who was peeved at our decision and determined to make us pay for our audacity. Less than an hour after leaving Christchurch, a thick plume of black smoke could be seen billowing from the back of the car."

"That was also an attempt at humour? You were an atheist and did not believe in the existence of any god. Is that not correct?"

"Yes Niara, I'm afraid it was just another futile attempt at being light-hearted. Shall I continue?"

"Please do."

"When I pulled over, I realised on closer inspection this was a terminal case. The motor had actually blown up on Christmas Day, possibly the worst time of the entire year to have something serious happen to a car. Fortunately, I had spare oil with me so, after topping up the oil, I was able to drive the remaining fifteen miles to Ashburton with black smoke practically enveloping the entire car.

"Upon arrival, I called into one of the motels and quizzed the owners as to who would be the most likely person to sell me a second hand engine, and secondly but just as importantly, who would be able to help me install it over the next day or two. As luck would have it, Ashburton was a medium sized town where everybody knew everyone else. The motel owners told me the bloke who owned the local wreckers was at a party. He gave me the phone number of the house where the party was being held as well as the phone number for a mechanic.

"This was in the days well before the advent of mobile phones, so contacting someone could be extremely difficult at times. After two or three attempts, I managed to get in touch with the wrecker who informed me he wasn't prepared to go back to the yard for a couple of days. However, he did have a solution for me. If I was willing to drop by the party and hand over $250, there was a complete Cortina engine just outside his wrecking yard that was mine for the taking.

"Doubt crept into my mind and I found myself asking 'Who would leave an engine on the outside of a yard unless it was worthless?'

"Before I could voice my concerns, the wrecker assured me the engine was in perfect working order and anyway it was the only engine he had that would fit my car. I found myself stuck between a rock and a hard place.

"I was positive the car had no chance of making it back to Christchurch in the condition it was in, and even if it did, I didn't have a clue when another car wrecker would be open. This was my one opportunity and I was going to take it. I raked up the necessary $250 from my ever-dwindling cash reserves for the purchase of the engine.

"It was still raining and I was concerned the car might break down completely at any moment, so we booked a motel room for the night. I left Laura there while I went to sort out the motor. The party was in full swing when I arrived but the wrecker was the first to the door on hearing my knock. As I handed over the money, he looked as if all his Christmases had come at once. He couldn't seem to wipe the smile from his face, probably thinking, 'It isn't every Christmas I'm paid $250 and get to screw an Australian at the same time.'

"After carefully counting the money, he gave me instructions as to where to find the engine and then bid me a fond adieu.

"I trundled off in my thick black smoke with the car hidden somewhere underneath and found the motor sitting in some long grass twenty minutes later. My next dilemma struck me. How the heck was I going to single-handedly pick up a complete motor and place it in the back of the station wagon?"

"How did you manage Grant? I would have imagined an engine to be quite heavy," asked Niara.

"Yes, you would think so, but being a brick layer had its advantages sometimes. We know how to keep things simple. I reasoned it was only four cylinders, not a big motor by any stretch of the imagination and I was quite a powerful person. I remember when I was doing my Clerk of Works course; the teacher would always single me out because of my very broad shoulders and large chest when talking about minimum sizes for manholes. Now it was time to put those shoulders to the test, stop thinking about it and just pick the bloody thing up. To my great amazement, I managed to do just that. It's incredible what you can achieve when you've run out of options."

"That is true Grant; the untapped power within is incredible. Please continue with your journey of misfortune."

"On the way back to the motel, I was so pleased with my efforts thus far that I initially failed to hear the police siren wailing behind me. Obviously, there was no chance of seeing him as the exhaust smoke obscured everything rearward and it wasn't until the police officer came up beside me, wildly gesticulating, that I managed to perceive he wanted me to pull over for a little chat."

"Driver, do you realise how much smoke is coming out of your car?"

"Yes, sorry Officer. My motor has just blown up today and as you can see, in the back (fortunately the smoke had dissipated enough so he could see into the back) I've found another motor and I'm going into town to organise a mechanic."

"My explanation appeared to fall on deaf ears as he continued to berate me for the next five minutes on how much of a nuisance my car and I were. Considering his was the only car I'd seen for the last hour, I didn't feel I'd been as much of a nuisance as he was making me out to be. Luckily, he must have decided a barrage of abuse was punishment enough and he didn't issue me with a fine. After he'd left, it made me think that perhaps I wasn't the only one in Ashburton having an unhappy Christmas Day.

"Back at the motel, I rang up the mechanic and managed to convince him Boxing Day was an ideal day to put a motor in a car. The next morning, we worked side by side, picking the best parts off both motors. We switched carburettors, distributors, coils and starter motors to rebuild one complete motor. Incredibly, just three hours later, we had the motor completely reassembled and fitted. Laura and I were in the car ready to go.

"We fired the engine up and more smoke came out of the exhaust than I was comfortable with, but the mechanic assured me it was likely due to condensation from the second hand motor sitting around for awhile. That was good enough for me and only twenty-four hours after the engine had originally blown up on Christmas Day, we were back on the road headed for Queenstown."

"Grant, I am sorry for interrupting you, especially from such an interesting tale of woe. However, I think you are missing the point," Niara said patiently.

"I'm sorry Niara. I know it's quite a long story but if you could please humour me, I'm sure once I've finished, my point will be crystal clear."

"Very well Grant, proceed."

"Thank you Niara."

"By the time we eventually did make Queenstown, a distance of three hundred miles from Ashburton, the car had already used a pint of oil. There was no escaping the fact; our new motor was seriously compromised. The question was, considering we weren't even half way around our circumnavigation of both islands, could we make it all the way back to Auckland before the second motor blew up? Only time was going to answer that conundrum.

"We had an absolute ball in Queenstown. The Shotover jet boat ride was one of the highlights. These jet propulsion boats reach speeds of up to fifty miles an hour and when we were heading for one of the sheer rock walls at that speed I was convinced the driver had miscalculated in his efforts to ensure a thrilling ride. When he finally threw the boat into a power slide, missing the wall by four inches and then raced to the next bend to do the exact same thing, I came to the conclusion he knew exactly what he was doing. The experience is definitely not for the faint hearted."

"I have seen these crafts before and they do look thrilling and quite dangerous. What was the next hardship?" Niara urged.

"Typically, the weather had set in again as we left Queenstown for the township of Dunedin. The lovely light drizzle that we'd come to appreciate had turned into a torrential downpour making driving difficult. We decided to stop and camp in the bushes, cooking in the car as it was too wet to get out. The next morning, I was about to light the gas stove for breakfast, when I realised more gas seemed to be coming out than usual. I decided to take it out into the middle of a clearing before lighting it, just in case.

"As soon as the match came close to the stove, it erupted into a ball of flame four feet high! The gas regulator had broken. I was relieved it hadn't broken the night before as we would have been incinerated in the car."

"You were fortunate not to get seriously injured Grant. What were your thoughts then?"

"I was thinking this was getting beyond ridiculous. As if I didn't have enough problems with the car, let alone having a gas bottle go on me as well. Later that morning, my makeshift repairs on the muffler finally gave way. Fortunately, it was nothing which more muffler bandage and wire couldn't fix. That was a lot more than could be said for the alternator when the warning light came on.

"The wrecker we managed to find in Dunedin explained that the alternator had burnt out due to water damage. The second hand replacement wasn't too expensive and in the end we only lost an hour of time. I wondered if this car would ever stop breaking down as I poured the daily pint of oil into it?

"My question was answered two days later after we reached our most southerly destination of Invercargill. The wheel alignment went out which was no big deal. Plenty of cars drive around with wheels misaligned all the time. Not this car though. It immediately scrubbed out the two front tyres making it dangerous to drive. I had just purchased some replacement tyres from the local wreckers when, surprise, surprise, the car wouldn't start. The starter motor had seized.

"By this time I didn't know whether to laugh or cry hysterically. This kind of thing only happened in movies. In real life this shouldn't be possible. The odds of this many breakdowns in one car over such a short period of time had to be a million to one. Yet, here I was again, once more placed in the unenviable position of trying to decide whether or not to part with more money for another replacement.

"There was no way out. I was trapped. I didn't have enough money to ditch this lemon and acquire another car. In fact, I would be lucky to have enough money to make it back to Auckland. I racked my mind for options and decided to do the only thing left I could think of. I reached into my back pocket and bought the f@&#n starter motor.

"Amazingly, the rest of the trip back to Auckland was fairly uneventful. The car used twenty pints of oil on the return trip but kept running. The only other part I had to replace was the radiator. I figured the car had finally run out of parts to break down. Incredibly, after six weeks, we still hadn't seen the sun. The locals kept telling us how unusual the weather was for this time of the year. We reckoned that's what the locals told all the tourists and you don't get a name like 'The Land of the Long White Cloud' for nothing.

"When we arrived back in Auckland, we headed straight for Kaye's home, the lovely lady we'd met on the ferry. We were down to our last few dollars and Kaye was kind enough to house us and more importantly, had a phone which people could contact us on when we advertised the car for sale. There must have been a real shortage of cheap vehicles as the phone didn't stop ringing. I sold it to the first person who came around for $1,000. What a relief it was to see that car gone and have some money again.

"The next day we caught the bus to Waitangi in the Bay of Islands. It was a beautiful area and we were fortunate enough to be there on Waitangi Day which celebrates the treaty signed with the native Maoris. There we finally saw the sun and it stayed with us for the remaining six days of our holiday. That was some trip.

"And you thought I couldn't problem-solve Niara? Huh!"

"Grant that was an incredible story. However, the problems you are able to solve and which you take such pride in are practical problems. The problems you need to solve and which are much harder are the problems within you. They are the problems that divide your psyche."

"What are you talking about? My whole life people have told me how well balanced and phlegmatic I am. What sort of inner problems do you think I could possibly have?"

"Your father for one," Niara responded.

I was taken aback for I had no retort.

"Grant, you have problems that are buried deep inside you. There will come a time when they must be released before you can progress. Again, nothing that is worthwhile is easy and this will be a momentous task for you, but I have faith that you will be able to endure and overcome these hurdles."

"What will happen if I can't?" I asked her.

The ensuing silence spoke a thousand words.

CHAPTER VIII

Unfortunately, Niara left me with nagging doubts while I was once more attempting to shift past my own light.

"I'm never going to cope with all this," I sighed.

If only Laura were here. I could discuss anything with her. We would bounce ideas and concepts off each other and inevitably come up with the best solution. We were always such a great team. It reminded me of the time when Laura and I started our relationship and we were put in a situation that if we hadn't worked as a team, there could have been tragic circumstances.

"Perhaps this story will have clues to help me on this Afterlife journey? I might even discover where I went wrong on Earth," I mused.

After renewing our friendship in that dusty campsite in Darwin, I discovered Laura had been having problems with her car. The next morning, I went down to the auto store, bought all the parts required to give the car a complete tune up and started working on it before Laura had risen. Imagine her surprise when within two hours, I had her little Datsun ready to scale mountains.

Our relationship started moving quickly after that. Who would have guessed the way to a girl's heart was through tuning her vehicle? Apparently, I had another attractive feature as well; a large aluminium slide-on camper which sat on the back of a Ford Falcon utility. With a fridge, oven, sink, dining table, a large comfortable double bed and best of all, flyscreens, made me almost irresistible. Laura had been camping pretty rough since arriving in Darwin.

Being in the tropical North, the temperature rarely dropped below twenty-six degrees Celsius and that's during the night. The days were far hotter. My dream girl was sheltered by an open lean-to with no mosquito nets and no mattress, just a sleeping bag on the hard ground. Her choice each night was to cover herself in the sleeping bag in a desperate bid to escape from a thousand mosquitoes or to boil to death in the humidity. No wonder I looked like a knight in shining armour. Who needs to look like Brad Pitt when you've got mosquito proofing?

We were spending virtually all our time together. We would often go into town of a morning and sit on the steps of the Vic Hotel waiting for it to open. Not to drink mind you, but to get inside one of the few buildings that had air-conditioning. It was glorious.

Six weeks after arriving in Darwin, we decided to do a short trip through Kakadu to the edge of Arnhem Land, down to Mataranka and then back up the highway to Darwin; a round trip of between four and five hundred miles. I rather liked the way the locals measured distances. They would convert miles to the amount of beer that would be consumed to complete a journey.

For instance, a trip of one hundred miles would probably take a bit under two hours and would equate to ten stubbies of beer, hopefully a bit less for the driver. That's equivalent to around three pints an hour. On considerably longer trips, miles were calculated in cartons of beer. North Territorians definitely knew how to drink.

About half way through our trip, we stopped at a billabong called Yellow Waters. At six miles long, with widths varying from ten to two hundred feet and chock a block full of barramundi fish and salt water crocodiles, it was an exhilarating place. We decided to go to a nearby pub for lunch and whilst there, we started chatting to a couple of guys who worked in the Jabiru uranium mine, a few hours' drive away. Gary was stockily built and around thirty years of age, while Rodney was of a slim build and in his early twenties, a similar age to us. They offered to take us with them on their boat for a fishing trip on the billabong that afternoon. We eagerly agreed and organised a time and place to meet before heading back to our campsite, completely unaware of the nightmare which awaited us…

So deep in thought was I, concentrating fully on my past experiences, I almost missed the moment I'd waited so long to achieve.

"YAHOO! I screamed into the nothingness.

At long last, I'd finally shifted past my own illumination. I didn't really understand how I'd achieved this miraculous result but I wasn't going to question it. I hazarded a guess it might have had something to do with all the practice being imprinted into my mind. My brain must have figured out how to shift when I'd allowed it to relax enough. The relief was amazing. It had been so hard to pick a spot in nothingness and then go there. I'd been trying for ages and it finally happened when I least expected it. Thrilled, I couldn't help but marvel how things could happen like that.

Metaphorically, I gave myself a pat on the back and decided to give myself a well-earned break for a little while before I started to practice my new found skill again. Almost with euphoria, I continued with my musings.

Catching up with the guys a few hours later, alarm bells should have been ringing when we noticed them loading a carton of beer into their sixteen foot tinnie along with the fishing gear. Beer, boats and crocodiles can be a very dangerous combination and unbeknown to us, these guys had continued drinking long after we had left them at the pub. After an hour of fishing without any luck and the boys drinking continuously, we tried to convince them it was time to head back before dark. To our relief, they agreed to return, but after they had tried just one more spot for ten minutes.

Laura and I were getting very concerned as Gary was driving exceedingly fast on waterways he wasn't overly familiar with and which contained many submerged logs. Thankfully, he managed to avoid any obstacles. Around ten minutes after arriving at the designated spot, just when we thought we could start heading home, Rodney hooked a barra and started reeling it in. By this stage, Gary was far drunker than any of us realised. He decided to stand up to net the barramundi. Incredibly, in his drunken stupor, he simply fell over, capsizing the boat in the process.

Salt water crocodiles are extremely dangerous at the best of times and this lagoon was absolutely full of them. We had already seen twenty of them in the short time we had been there. To make matters worse, it was breeding season and they were far more aggressive than usual. I later discovered that the area where we had capsized, very near the end of the billabong, was home to a breeding pair with the male estimated at nearly eighteen feet long.

We all managed to struggle to the shore, if that's what you could call it, only to discover it was actually bottomless marsh mud which you would sink into past your knees and was extremely difficult to move around on.

After a few minutes of serious deliberations, it was decided that the only solution to our dilemma was to retrieve the boat which was now upside down on the surface of the water. Going back in was one of the most unnerving experiences one could ever imagine. Treading water, expecting at any moment to feel a vice like grip somewhere on your body and to be dragged under and ripped apart, was the stuff of nightmares. It only took a few minutes to recover the boat but it felt like hours.

Once back on shore, after we'd bailed the remaining water out, we realised we'd lost everything. There were no oars or rollicks, no torches and the motor was water damaged and unworkable. The only thing we still had was Rodney's fishing rod with the fish still attached. It was getting dark and we knew we were in a lot of danger.

All along the edge of this part of the lagoon grew huge bamboo style plants, fifteen feet high and four inches in diameter. I thought we could use one of them to push the boat along, gondola style, similar to the way boats are manoeuvred in Venice. Alas, no such luck. The mud beneath the water was bottomless and I was unable to find a purchase point for the pole. The only other option we had left was to use two of the poles as oars, but without rollicks or blades attached to the poles, the progress was going to be painfully slow. To make matters worse, Gary was so drunk and disorientated, he became convinced we were going in the wrong direction and refused to help.

That's when I first got to see the true mettle within Laura's petite frame. The only way we were able to make any progress at all was to have two rowers side by side. Each rower had to hold their piece of bamboo in both hands and glide it through the water in much the same action as a dog would paddle. If one rower stopped, the boat would turn in circles. With

Gary sitting near the motor swearing at us and refusing to row, it was left up to Rodney and me.

Unbelievably, this young man had no mental strength and had to stop every few minutes to rest. By now, it had become so dark I couldn't see the person sitting beside me. I tried to put my hand right up to my face but I couldn't see it. Apart from where I was now, I had never experienced such complete darkness. To exacerbate the problems, every so often we'd hear another crocodile slither into the water. Each time it happened, we were left wondering if that reptile would be the one which would attack the boat.

After an hour of going nowhere, Laura took over from Rodney and we finally started making some slow progress. Laura rowed non-stop for five hours under some of the toughest conditions imaginable. Gary steadfastly refused to help during the entire ordeal and at times became so agitated I was convinced he was going to capsize the boat again. Each time this happened, we managed to humour him with the promise of a carton of beer if we were going the wrong way. In the back of my mind though all I could think was,

"When we get safely back to shore, I'm going to beat you to a pulp, you dumb bastard."

Even though we were heading in the right direction, we still had another major problem to overcome. How to find the camping ground in this pitch blackness? Potentially, we could row right past it and find ourselves at the other end of the lagoon. By now it was after midnight and we were at the end of our energy reserves.

Fortunately for us, we had an incredible piece of good luck. We saw car headlights about half a mile away. The only place it made sense for those lights to be was the campsite. Now if they'd only leave the lights on we'd be able to find our way there. Oh no, they've turned the lights off!

I screamed out into the darkness, "Turn your lights back on, we're lost. Turn your lights back on!"

After two more shouts of desperation… relief. They'd heard me and the lights flickered back on. It still took a further forty-five minutes to reach the campground and occasionally we'd call out to reassure the driver we were still coming.

By the time we reached the shore, I was so relieved that we had made it back alive, my anger had completely dissipated. Rodney blamed the disaster on the fish he'd caught and insisted we take it. We profusely thanked the guy who'd left his lights on for so long and then Laura and I headed to the camper and put ourselves to bed. Sleep escaped us for the entire night. We kept re-living every detail over and over again. Both of us realised how lucky we were, not only to survive, but to also have each other.

Laura proved that day what a truly exceptional human being she was. Her calm demeanour, incredible stamina and mental strength, were a wonder to behold. Over the next forty years, she proved these wonderful attributes time and time again. Not many men could be so lucky as to have a partner like Laura.

"Where are you now Laura? Are you safe and well back on Earth? Don't worry, we'll meet again one day," I promised.

Only a few months later, we were in Cairns for a week and decided to venture further up north to the Daintree area. Whilst there, we met a lovely lady who worked at the local post office. She was easy to talk to and we described our close call with the crocodiles at Yellow Waters. After listening to our story, she reassured us that we probably weren't in as much danger as we'd imagined. In fact, she told us, she and her family regularly swam in a section of river known to have salt water crocodiles frequent it. Tragically, Beryl Wruck was attacked and killed by a crocodile just a year later while standing in her favourite bathing area late one night.

I was surprised how all these thoughts would drift through my mind, yet I wasn't convinced any of them were helping me get closer to discovering my purpose or where I went wrong. I'd been bouncing around in my space for ages now and I was finding it quite weird. I could go in any direction endlessly and yet I haven't come across one other being or solid object. The ability to move is so effortless now, I hardly feel like I am focusing at all. Gratefully, I realised this has given me even more opportunity to think of other things, my children being one of them. I couldn't help but wonder if perhaps the answers lay there."

We had our second child, a son whom we named Chase, when I was thirty-two. I was building a new house for us at the time. Eight years later, we had a surprise visitor in the form of a little girl we named Skye. I mentally laughed aloud at the memory of how Skye had come about.

Laura, Casey, Chase and I had gone on a week-long ski trip to Perisher Valley. My mate Steve, his wife, Ebony and their son, Will, had joined us. Richard, his daughter, Charity and her sister Peta, along with their mothers Brenda and Karra, completed the group.

There wasn't much snow at the time and within the first two hours I'd fallen heavily and damaged the acromioclavicular joint in my shoulder. The doctor informed me that I wouldn't be able to ski for the week as, if I fell again, I would risk permanent injury to my shoulder which might prevent me from laying bricks for a long time.

My chairlift ticket was worth a few hundred dollars and fortunately I was able to give it to Steve, as he hadn't purchased a ticket yet. I was raving on to Steve how well everything had turned out, with him not having a ticket and all. He said he felt like shaking me. Didn't I get it? My whole holiday was ruined and there was no bright side.

But he was wrong; Laura would pop in each day for an hour or so to keep me company while everyone was skiing. Nine months later, Skye came into our lives, so there ended up being a huge bright side. Even Skye's birth was a real family affair with both Casey and Chase witnessing her arrival.

That holiday with Richard present, reminded me of another holiday I'd shared with him years earlier, before Chase or Skye were born. Richard, Laura, Casey and I did a trip around the world for four months. Casey was only eighteen months old at the time and everyone thought we were insane.

"How are you and Laura going to manage, cooped up together with a toddler and a gay man who has no experience with looking after a kid?" friends would say. "You'll all be at each other's throats in no time. You're asking for disaster."

I will admit it did start off a little disastrously. The plane was packed and as we didn't have to pay for Casey because of her age, it meant we would have to nurse her for the entire thirteen hour flight. Two hours out and the plane developed an electrical problem and had to return to the airport. Once we'd landed, we weren't allowed to disembark as the airport terminal was closed. It took six hours to repair the problem before we were finally able to restart the journey. By the time we finally made it to Heathrow Airport in England, Casey had been sitting on our laps for nearly twenty-four hours. Talk about a marathon start.

Another thing which made that European trip a little harder than normal was Laura's insistence we only use cloth nappies. Laura had always been a greeny and couldn't stand the environmental damage disposable nappies created. Even though we were travelling the world and seeing all these amazing sights, didn't mean we could avoid cleaning shitty nappies every day. And she stuck to her guns; we never bought one bag of disposable nappies for the entire trip.

Richard proved to be more than capable of dealing with a toddler and was fantastic with Casey, although there were definitely times when he was reaching his limit. One day, Richard had spent all morning washing and drying a fresh white shirt. Whilst Richard was sitting in the front seat, Casey decided to give him a cuddle from behind. Unfortunately, half the banana she was carrying broke off and slid down Richard's neck, only to get squashed between Richard's back and the seat, leaving Richard with a sticky back and a dirty shirt for the rest of the day. He was not amused.

Our overseas sojourn was a lesson to us all regarding differences in how people think and behave. We thought we'd seen it all back home but we were to find out otherwise. The recollections of our encounters in Scotland became family favourites for the re-telling.

The pictures in my mind, of the laughter we shared every time we related our experiences, created cheerful warmth within me.

"Those were the days," I pondered warmly.

Ever the optimist, I could only hope that maybe one day, somehow, we'd all be together again to share those interesting times...

It was late one afternoon when we arrived at Pitgrudy Farm, a caravan park near Dornoch, Scotland. We were immediately met by the owners, an elderly couple, who proceeded to quiz us. They asked one of the strangest questions we'd been asked on our trip so far.

"Ya hud a shower teday?"

Startled, we all responded with, "Yes, we all showered this morning."

"Then ya dinna need to use the showers tonight," he stated purposefully.

"Hold on a moment, we've been driving all day and will need to freshen up," I explained.

He grunted and shook his head, clearly displeased with my response but he left it at that.

After we had set up the campervan, we decided to have a look around. We were impressed by how spotless everything was and surprised that, apart from the owner's caravan and our campervan, there was only one other vehicle in the entire campground. We were also amazed at the amount of signage around. Nearly everything had a sign on it.

All the taps had either 'don't touch' or 'make sure this is turned off' and the same with any switches. Even the windows had signs on them warning people to leave them alone. Other signs commanded not to take any of the hot water, while another directed that you couldn't do your laundry in the amenities block. In fact, there were so many signs I started to convince myself I was part of the 'Alice in Wonderland' story!

When Laura was looking through the window of the laundry, the old lady came racing out of her caravan screaming, "Ya canna do your laundry in thar, the laundry's loched."

Laura tried to explain that she was just looking and didn't need to do any laundry today but the old lady was too agitated to hear.

"It's loched, it's loched, ya canna do ya laundry here," she carried on, spittle flying everywhere as she stood blocking the locked door.

She wouldn't move until Laura had walked well away.

A little later, Richard decided to have a shower. I have to admit Richard's toiletry bag was rather over-sized and it was obviously big enough to concern the old man. Richard had made it half-way to the amenities block when the old man came shuffling out of his caravan as fast as he could go.

"Ya canna do your laundry in thar, ya canna do your laundry in thar."

Richard assured him he was going for a shower, not to do laundry.

"What have ya got in tha bag than?" he persisted.

"Just my toiletries," Richard responded.

"It's ta big for that."

"Well, that's all I have so if you'll excuse me...?" and Richard headed off, leaving his antagonist spluttering.

Every night after dinner, we'd put Casey to bed and have a few games of something or other. Usually it was Monopoly, Canasta or another card game called 'Rickety Kate', a variation of Hearts. This one particular night, it was after eleven before we'd finished our game and we still hadn't done the dishes. Deciding speed was of the essence, I chose to ignore the many signs which said I couldn't take any hot water from the amenities block. I was sure that in the darkness and because of the late hour, I would have zero chances of being caught.

With kettle in hand, I had taken no more than five paces from our campervan when the old man came hurtling out of his caravan yelling at the top of his voice, "Ya canna take any hot water. Stop! Ya canna have any hot water."

I was so stunned I could only reply with an "Oh, sorry!" and turned back to the campervan, tail between my legs.

To this day, I still don't know how he could see I was carrying a kettle. Their caravan was at least two hundred feet from ours and it was very dark. Obviously, they had been watching us and had probably decided they wouldn't go to bed until our lights were off. Or perhaps they had a pair of night vision glasses or a listening device that caught our conversation when discussing getting the hot water?

That incident remained one of the great unsolved mysteries of my life. Who knows? I might meet them here at some time and finally discover the truth.

"I wonder if Niara could organise something like that?" popped into my mind.

A week later we were preparing to cross over to the Isle of Skye. We were travelling late in the season so there weren't many tourists about. We'd pulled up in an extremely large car park which would normally cater for over five hundred vehicles but was virtually empty at the time. As Richard and I were discussing whether he should do some shopping before we crossed to Skye, a short, stocky Scotsman, about thirty years of age, came bellowing up to our van.

"Ya canna park your van thar, ya canna park ya van thar," he repeated in his thick Scottish accent.

Unruffled, I answered with "Excuse me, I'm talking at the moment," and proceeded to finish my conversation with Richard, all the while with this man standing at my door repeating over and over that I couldn't park there.

I must admit to being a bit confused by his sense of urgency as the only other car in the entire car park was way over the other side, in a position which suggested it was owned by one of the workers, while our car was parked in one of five hundred clearly marked bays with the motor still running as we had only been there a minute before he'd come over.

Richard jumped out to do the shopping, so I explained to the man that I wanted to catch the ferry to Skye and did he know the process of acquiring a ticket. He loudly and abruptly said,

"Ya park in the queue and get ya ticket thar," pointing to nowhere in particular.

With that he walked off and stopped about three hundred feet away. Mystified, as I couldn't discern any queue to get into, I decided to drive over to him and attempt to glean some more information.

When I pulled the car up next to him he said "Yes?" and acted as if we'd never met or had a conversation before.

I managed to blurt out "I want to go to Skye…" but before I could say another word, he handed me a ticket saying "That will be twelve pound, fifty pence."

I looked at him incredulously thinking, "This is just like a Monty Python movie! Why didn't he just give me a ticket in the first place?"

The little Scotsman brought me back to earth when he started yelling,

"Okay, move on, move on!" gesticulating wildly as he urged me onto the ferry. "Hold on," I cried out to the Scotsman. "My brother's not back yet. How long will it be before the ferry leaves?"

"Twenty-five minutes," he lied. "Now move on!"

I thought that would give Richard plenty of time, as he was only buying a few items, so I did as I had been told and drove on. Within thirty seconds, I felt the ferry start to shift and then we were off, leaving Richard and the shoreline behind us. When Richard returned, we were nowhere to be seen. After a short search, he decided to ask our Scottish friend if he knew the whereabouts of our van.

"Excuse me; have you seen where our blue van went?" Richard asked politely.

The little Scotsman turned around and putting his face close to Richard's, yelled at the top of his voice, "WHAT BLUE VAN?"

Stepping back, Richard replied, "You know! The one you were talking to my brother in."

"I DON'T KNOW!" he screamed and abruptly turned and walked away.

Fortunately, another worker who had observed everything took pity on Richard and managed to relay three words to him as he too walked away.

"It's gorn over."

Richard was in a quandary as to how to get to Skye. With no-one else prepared to offer any information, he eventually found a notice board which explained walking passengers were able to ride the ferry for free and the service ran every fifteen minutes. Within the hour, Richard was on the Isle of Skye and rejoicing with us. Having had two extremely unpleasant encounters with Scots within the first week of our travel in that beautiful country, we became convinced public relations weren't one of Scotland's strong points.

Thinking of my family made me wonder how long ago it had been since I had died. It could be a year or a couple of years. I really wouldn't have a clue. Both my birth and marriage families may be dead for all I knew. I'm amazed that not once have I missed them in a sorrowful way. I'm happy that every thought I have of them is only one of joy. It's as if all sad thoughts are blocked. I had a great deal of happiness in my life back on Earth but it's still nothing to the highs I feel here.

Suddenly Niara appeared. For the first time since I'd met her, Niara's calm reserve seemed to be slightly shaken. I couldn't put my finger on it but I knew something was wrong.

"Has something happened Niara?"

"That is very perceptive of you Grant. However, it is nothing which would concern you," she responded bluntly.

"I'm sorry Niara. I don't want to pry. However, by you not telling me, it will make me more concerned, not less."

"Very well Grant. You will hear about it soon enough so I see no harm. Many people on Earth are in a perilous situation; literally millions are dying every day."

"What are you saying? What has happened?" I asked, immediately starting to worry about my own family. Were they in danger?

Niara replied, "Let me explain what has led up to these events so you may better understand the tragedy we are now facing. The population has finally expanded to an unsustainable amount. There are fifteen billion people on the planet now. The Governments were struggling to feed most of the people as it was, then seven years ago a worldwide drought started. All the crops withered and died before turning to dust; the rain and monsoons never came. The drought is still going with no end in sight.

"The water shortage has become so critical that any crops earmarked for animals have been diverted to feed humans. All the piggeries, poultry farms and dairies have closed and the animals destroyed through lack of feed. Beef cattle had already being reduced due to the ongoing methane problem. Now, without water, they are being decimated.

"The planet has overheated, ice caps have melted and consequently, ocean levels have risen. Many countries have been inundated and the world's land mass has been reduced.

"Bangladesh has lost more than half its land and over seven hundred million people have been displaced. Countless other countries are suffering the same fate. Most of the islands in the Pacific and Indian oceans have become uninhabitable. The Maldives were lost completely. The countries which could afford it have built massive levees to try and protect their land from the rising seas but they do not know what height the ocean levels will reach, or whether their levees will hold.

"With the critical shortage of food and natural resources, the most severe drought ever recorded and the huge financial drain on every country, businesses started to crack under the strain. The ensuing stock market crash placed all the developed countries into a depression more severe than the '1929 Great Depression'.

"Two years ago, all these factors triggered the largest human migration in history. Africa had an exodus of over a billion people into Europe. Each country tried to contain their borders, but with their own internal problems such as rioting, food shortages, skyrocketing prices and very high unemployment, they were overcome by a never-ending sea of desperate people.

"Your country of birth, Australia, became a primary target for many Asian countries. Owing to Australia's vast coastline, it was unable to contain its borders. With over one hundred thousand people arriving daily, small seaside towns were overrun within hours and local authorities were killed. Within the first six months, the Australian Government had been overtaken. In less than two years, Australia's population of forty million was displaced by one hundred and fifty million refugees.

"The United States Government was one of the last countries to succumb. With refugees coming via Mexico and Canada and a never ending flotilla of humanity attacking both coastlines, the end was inevitable. The only way the Government maintained any control was by locking themselves away in their heavily fortified bunkers, but their six hundred million constituents were left to fend for themselves. Life is chaos with almost all industries collapsing, no law and order and not enough food. A whole new class of people have been created. The people who could still afford to eat meat versus the grain eaters. Many wealthy people were killed simply for the meat they had stockpiled.

"Eventually, the top four nations had a secret meeting on how to deal with the dilemma. It was agreed the population had to be decreased rapidly. They secretly introduced a new strain of extremely contagious smallpox virus to various third world countries with devastating effects. Within the first month, one thousand people had died. By the end of the second month, this had increased to twenty thousand deaths and by year's end; one billion people had died with no signs of abating. The virus spread so rapidly, that within eighteen months it occupied virtually every country in the world. This is genocide on a scale we have never experienced before. Grant, we do not know how it will all end. Humankind is facing its greatest peril."

"I don't understand Niara. How could all this happen so quickly? When I died, there weren't even seven billion on the planet, let alone fifteen billion. This story sounds insane. None of it is making any SENSE," I exploded.

It was then that Niara dropped the final bombshell.

"Grant, it is the year 2062 on Earth. You died fifty years ago."

CHAPTER IX

Shock numbed me. "That can't be!" was all I could gasp.

A huge wave of unreality swept over me. "Fifty years, fifty years, fifty years, fifty years," kept drumming over and over in my head in an endless, horrifying rhythm.

I couldn't have moved even if I'd wanted to. Why didn't I know? Why couldn't I guess? How had I not felt so much passage of time had passed? A vortex of emotions rolled inside me. It had been bad enough when Niara had told me about being here ten months. The same feelings and thoughts coursed through me as then but tripled in intensity. The only oil on my troubled waters was the ever-soothing music.

"What about my family?" I managed to croak, but there was no answer.

Even the all-pervasive peace which surrounded me couldn't compete with the horrors my mind now conjectured. As the information Niara had relayed sunk in, my brain recoiled at the thought of the waste and needless loss of life, the awful suffering so many had endured. I hoped my family had died quickly and were at peace, not caught in the terror which had engulfed humanity.

Where had it gone wrong? Humankind had appeared to be on the brink of unlocking all the secrets of life. Living should have been a glorious achievement by now, not this dreadful scenario. I'd envisaged cures for ill health, no more poverty and equality for all. Knowledge should have been Man's saving grace. Where was all that knowledge now?

Interrupting my thoughts, Niara began to speak again.

"Grant, I have come to say goodbye. I may not see you again."

Niara's words were solemn and something like apprehension resonated in her voice, alerting me to the fact that Niara was battling to keep her emotions in check. A sick feeling wended its way through my innermost parts.

"Why not?" was all I managed to expel, trepidation mounting like rising water in a flood.

"As dreadful as the situation is on Earth, there is a far greater problem occurring here," Niara responded unhappily. "I had no wish to burden you with our problem. I merely wished to have the opportunity to speak words of farewell and convey my hopes that you will enjoy your transitions."

"Niara, you said 'our' problem. Aren't I part of the 'our'? Surely I have a right to know what is happening. Please tell me," I coaxed.

"Oh Grant," she shuddered. "Yes, you do have a right to know. As you are now aware, the energy which was gifted to you as life from Nyame returns at death, an uncorrupted energy to the transitions and a corrupted energy to destruction. This has been the way since the beginning of mankind and there have been no problems. Now however, the influx of energies is so great that the portal between Earth and the first stage transition cannot accommodate the masses. They are colliding and destroying each other. We are losing thousands of valuable essences," Niara cried despairingly.

"I don't understand what you're saying Niara. You're not making any sense. How can they possibly be killing each other? I wasn't aware of anything until I'd arrived here. I had no conscious thoughts. Are these essences different? Is this like rats off a sinking ship, a stampede trying to escape the horrors of Earth? Do they think there will only be room for a chosen few?" I questioned, my distress increasing with every thought.

"Calm yourself Grant," Niara ordered. "There is not much time but I will attempt to explain. The energies are unaware of each other. They are simply following the route to Nyame, which means they must travel through the opening to this place. The portal is a wormhole, an opening in the fabric of space much like a black hole without the massive gravitational forces acting on it. At the centre, the wormhole is minuscule, but certainly large enough to handle any previous influx which has occurred throughout history. This, however, is unprecedented continuous volume and the wormhole cannot cope.

"Each deceased human's energy has something like a force field surrounding it. This is a protection for the essence whilst it travels to Nyame in its unawakened state. Normally, the strength of this field repels anything which comes near, but now, with so many flowing through the wormhole; they are being funnelled in too closely and then wedged in like sardines. Compression creating heat occurs, which sparks a chain reaction similar to a mini supernova. At each blast, thousands of perfectly good essences are lost forever. Even as we speak, many are meeting with oblivion," Niara groaned.

"Grant, these people will never get a second chance. They will have lost their immortality forever. We must find a way to slow the rate of deaths on Earth. The loss of these energies may very well affect the future," Niara declared. "It is absolutely necessary that life on Earth is preserved. If humankind becomes extinct, I fear for us all."

For a fleeting second, my mind lingered on why mankind's existence was so necessary, but there were too many other issues taking priority. My thoughts went into overdrive. If my family were dead, as I'd hoped they were to avoid the abhorrent situation on our home planet, they could very well be amongst the travellers to the portal and therefore be in imminent danger.

I shied away from the idea of the many annihilated ones. I couldn't bear to think of my family being totally lost for eternity. I had received this gift of immortality, something I'd never believed possible, and now I desperately wanted that same gift for my loved ones. I couldn't stand the thought that all the people I had held dear in my life would be denied the opportunity to experience the Afterlife.

"What can be done Niara? Can this tragedy be averted?"

"Many of the Guides have volunteered to return to Earth. We will find the vaccine, vary it to kill the more virulent strain, process enough for the remaining population and distribute it. It is the hope that if we can act quickly enough, humankind will be saved. It is a terrible risk. Any time that the course of history on Earth is interfered with, places and events in the future can be compromised," Niara concluded, worry colouring her words with all its nuances of doubt, alarm and fretfulness.

"Let me help Niara. Let me go back with you!" I implored.

"Grant, you do not realise what you are offering or what dangers you would face. No, it is impossible. You have not yet even progressed to your therapy. You would be too great a burden for me at a time when I would need to have my wits about me.

"The Guides must return through the same worm hole. If any of us get trapped amongst the incoming masses, we will suffer the same fate and we will also perish. Many of us will not be returning after this mission. It is almost impossible to get through, which is why I wanted to come and say 'Kwaheri'. Farewell and goodbye in my former Earth language," she whispered.

"Niara, you said it was nearly impossible to get through. Does this mean there is still a possibility of making it back to Earth?" I asked, clutching at every straw.

"Yes Grant, with timing and good fortune I believe that there may be a way," she replied slowly and I could envisage the wheels of her mind turning, prospecting through the various methods she might employ to find a solution.

"Please Niara, I beg you. Please let me come with you. I want to help. I need to help."

"Grant, I feel your need and I would like to accommodate your wishes but you are my responsibility and this mission is too fraught with danger to risk your eternal life."

"What good is my eternal life if I spend it knowing I hadn't tried to help my family and others achieve their eternal lives?" I questioned her bitterly. "A million years filled with a billion tears is useless to me. Niara, I'd far rather perish than sit here safely while hundreds of thousands are doomed. I don't know what I can do, but I know I can do something."

I felt her resolve beginning to weaken and pounced.

"Niara, you are my Guide, not my owner. It should be my decision whether I stay or go."

She was quiet for long moments and tension rippled the air between us. At last she broke the silence.

"Normally, I would not entertain the thought of someone as inexperienced as you undertaking this journey," Niara replied quietly, almost as if she was talking aloud to herself. "However, perhaps your lack of experience here and only recently leaving Earth could be an advantage."

Niara stopped and waited, seemingly transfixed. Finally she spoke, but it seemed she was addressing herself, not me.

"I have received no negative reaction."

Her voice strengthened as she made her decision.

"I will allow you to come on two conditions. Firstly, you must never leave my side. Secondly, you must act on my instructions immediately and without question. Failure to do so will almost certainly cost you your life," she warned.

"Thank you Niara. I promise you won't regret this. I swear to you that I will do as I am instructed, unquestionably and instantly. When do we leave?" I asked, fearful of giving her the time to change her mind.

"Immediately," was her brusque and unexpected response. "Many of the Guides are already waiting by the worm hole. I have tarried far too long in my desire to inform you of my departure. I will implant an image within you of the entrance to the worm hole. You will need to project yourself there. If you fail to do so, I shall not wait or return for you," she stated icily. "Receive the image and project yourself now!"

A picture flashed into my mind and I willed myself towards it with every ounce of my being. Instantly, I was transported to the spot, a large, rotating hole in the fabric of space. To me, it looked like a huge funnel lying on its side. The exterior of the orifice was a yellowish white while the interior, or what I could see of it, was a foreboding black. It was hard to see inside because of the pale, newborn Auras streaming from its innermost parts like a beautiful cascading fireworks display; a kaleidoscope of colours all flowing in one direction. In morbid fascination I watched, aghast at the never-ending volume of dead and wondered if any of my dear ones were amongst this vast multitude.

I sensed no thought or feeling from any of them. Trance-like, they streamed ever closer to Nyame and the first transition, blindly being pulled like iron shavings to a magnet.

"At least these are the lucky ones who will have a chance," I comforted myself, overwhelmed at witnessing the tangible evidence of what had been happening on the Earth. I could have wept at such a terrible loss of life and the suffering these people had undergone before death had claimed them.

I glanced at Niara and was shocked beyond belief.

"Niara, you have a form!"

I could see the ghostly outline of a female body.

"Yes, our aural energy leaves a faint imprint of the body we leave behind on Earth. It stays with us forever."

"Why couldn't I see it before now and why don't I have one?"

"The reason why you could not see my image before is because the void is too dark to see such a faint outline and as to your second question, you do have an imprint. You just need to look harder."

I imagined putting my hand out in front of me and sure enough, the faint outline of my hand appeared.

"Wow! That's awesome."

After a quick investigation, I decided I was far more interested in looking at Niara's shape than my own.

I could now see that the two twinkling stars formed part of her eyes and the colourful band above them could almost be mistaken for hair. Her nose was broader than most Caucasians but in perfect proportion to her face. She had high cheekbones and her lips were beautiful and full. Her neck was long and slender atop what appeared to be a lithe, athletic body. There was something special about her which I couldn't quite put my finger on, almost as if she was royalty.

"She would have been stunning to look at in the flesh," I thought as Niara broke the spell.

"We must hurry Grant. We may move through the wormhole freely here. Follow me."

Once inside, I saw hundreds of Guides heading against the continuous flow of former humanity. The Guides looked like an army of ghosts disappearing into a black cavern. Joining them, we floated along the ever-narrowing corridor of space. Up ahead, every few seconds I could see a flash of blinding light followed by a sizzling, cracking sound.

"What's happening Niara?" I whispered, trying to keep the trepidation out of my voice.

"That is the narrowest point ahead, Grant. You must be exceedingly careful not to be drawn in. This is where the energies are being compressed and suffering destruction," she replied tensely.

Drawing ever closer, the problem became clearly evident. The Auras were truly packed in like sardines. It was as if there was a terrible traffic pile-up with horrendous results. Even as we watched, we could see the build-up of heat and energy. It felt as if we were waiting for a volcano to erupt.

Suddenly, there was a mind-numbing explosion and the energies at the centre were obliterated, freeing the wormhole for a matter of seconds, allowing thousands of Auras through until the incoming tide jammed new ones tight again. It was sickening and absolutely fear-inspiring. It didn't take long before the whole process repeated itself and it appeared that the ones getting through were equalled by the ones being destroyed.

"Watch as the Guides time their run Grant. They must get through and past the incoming Auras before the passage blocks again. There is no escape. If they are caught, they will perish. Once they get through, they will make their way to the end of the worm hole and then project themselves to Earth."

"Why can't they just project themselves to Earth from here?"

"There is no projection through the wormhole. It is the control station in and out of the transitions. It is a safeguard against any unforeseen surprises," explained Niara.

Fleetingly, I thought to question her further but decided against it. I needed to focus on the task ahead. Steeling myself, I watched as the Guides, ten at a time, lined up, waited for the ordeal of the explosion and then quickly floated through the ensuing gap. Two groups made the difficult navigation. Soon it would be our turn. I watched and tried to prepare myself for the timing of my run.

Everything seemed to be progressing smoothly until the sixth group made their attempt. As they were making their way through, one Guide appeared to be knocked off balance by a cluster of Auras coming from the opposite direction. He, in turn, was pushed into another Guide. The mishap only cost both of them one or two seconds but it was enough. Before they could progress any further, they were surrounded and completely engulfed by the Auras. They were hopelessly snared.

I mentally reached out to connect with them, anguish ripping and tearing at me, only to find myself being drawn into the death trap.

"Let go or you will also perish!" Niara demanded hoarsely.

As painful as it was, my reaction was instant and I released contact, springing back to Niara's side. Almost all colour seemed to have drained from her. The colour of her aura was virtually white and I felt her pain wounding me.

"You cannot help them Grant. This is the sacrifice they were prepared to make and they are doing it with peace in their minds. This may also be our fate. I have lived many thousands of years in the Afterlife and I am prepared to forego my place in the scheme of Nyame, but you Grant, need not do this. There is no shame if you should change your mind and return to your transition," she offered me gently.

"I will not leave," I managed to choke out before the explosion occurred which wiped out the Guides.

Niara's distress was tangible and I could feel the love that she held for them.

"Who were they?" I asked as comfortingly as I could.

"They were Anka and Quiling, Guides I have known for a very long time. Their beauty shone within them," she replied, so softly I could barely pick up her thoughts.

Slowly, colour returned to her and with it her usual all-pervading calmness. And boy, I sure needed her calmness now. The death of Anka and Quiling had completely rattled me and seriously shaken my confidence. Our turn was next.

"When I tell you to go, do not hesitate Grant," Niara ordered.

Sickening dread filled me but I resolved to do this no matter what the consequence. Suddenly there was another flash and I heard Niara's urgent,

"Go now!"

I floated quickly and smoothly into the rift, keeping Niara in view at all times. We passed through the narrow neck and then, for the first time, I was confronted with the full frontal image of a wall of Auras bearing down on me. I lost sight of Niara, panicked and froze.

"Keep moving! Go through them!" I heard her scream shrilly in my head.

It was just what I needed. It impelled me forward. I knew I dare not stop to look for Niara and forged ahead, forcing my way through the seething wall of prospective Beings.

After what seemed an eternity, the tunnel became larger and I was able to move more freely. It was with utter relief I saw Niara waiting just outside the tunnel entrance.

"Well done Grant," were her first words and I noted the relief and a hint of pride in her voice.

"You have made it through the first major hurdle. Now we must project ourselves to Earth. Our target is a secure laboratory in the State Research Centre of Virology and Biotechnology Vector in Koltsovo, Russia.

"It is one of two remaining strongholds for the smallpox virus and vaccine and it is guarded by armed troops at all times. More importantly, the laboratory has the ability to mass produce. I will plant the destination in your mind and you must follow as before."

Obeying instinctively, I received the image and willed myself forward. In a flash I was back on Earth. Harsh reality hit me as I looked around the unfamiliar surroundings. Death and misery were everywhere. Bodies were piled up in the streets, a feast for clouds of blowflies. The stench was pervasive and disgusting. Sick and dying lay groaning where they had fallen, their faces masks of anguish and pain.

I watched as a young girl, perhaps five years old, wandered the street. She looked dehydrated and malnourished. She was sobbing but it was as if she didn't have enough moisture left in her body to produce tears. It was heartbreaking to see her walking around, calling for her mother. Not a single person so much as glanced at her.

The infected people looked horrific. It was clear from the black, unclotted blood oozing from their mouths and other orifices, and the flailing skin hanging from their bodies, that they were suffering from the most extreme and deadly variation of smallpox, blackpox. I had read about this strain once before when I was alive. The virus destroys the linings of the throat, the stomach, the intestines, the rectum and the vagina as well as the exterior and interior linings of the skin. It is virtually one hundred percent fatal.

Pitifully, the ill reached out to the ones still unaffected by the disease but fear prevented the healthy offering any help. Instead, they wandered aimlessly around with haunted expressions of despair etched onto their faces, unable to deal with the daily nightmare that confronted them. Most shops had been broken into and looted with the shelves now completely bare. It was obvious that both food and clean water were in scarce supply.

Two starving dogs were trying to eat a human carcass but it appeared as if the flesh was too putrid even for them to digest. As quickly as they swallowed a piece of meat, they would vomit it back up. Their eyes were completely glazed over and without water; I would have been surprised if they lasted another twenty-four hours. All the trees and grass were brown and dead. Even the weeds couldn't survive. An air of hopelessness hung over everything and everyone. Niara jolted me from my repugnant survey.

"It has not been attempted often but the Guides need to take over the bodies of as many humans as we can find who are suitable for our task. These chosen ones must have a selfless spirit to allow us entry. Any who are hard-hearted are untenable," she informed me.

"But how do I know who is suitable and how do I enter their body?"

"It is much like when you are projecting yourself to a place. You must relax and think yourself there. A welcoming soul will allow you entry and will be nurtured by your close proximity. Those who are hedonistic, self-centred, cruel or thoughtless will have a barrier around themselves you will not be able to penetrate. It will be like hitting a proverbial brick wall. But then, you would be used to that would you not Grant, having been a bricklayer once upon a time?" she commented dryly.

"Oh Niara!" was all I could find to say and I allowed myself a tiny smile in this brutal place.

Somehow that small piece of humour settled me more than a thousand words could have. I listened intently as Niara resumed speaking.

"Grant, you must practise on a lower life form before you attempt to enter a human. Start with something small because a larger animal may be harder for you to manipulate until you have gained mastery of the energy over-ride."

With that sage piece of advice ringing in my ears, Niara disappeared to begin her search area.

"Hmm, now what am I going to try this on?" I wondered, before almost immediately spying a group of ants scurrying across the footpath. "Well, you can't get too much smaller than these guys, that's for sure."

I let myself relax as Niara had suggested and thought myself into the body of the nearest little insect. It was quite a pleasant feeling, almost as if I was melting from something solid into something liquid or I had become the steam after having been the boiling pot of water. I guess that's why the culmination of the process was such a shock.

Though now an Aura, my mind was definitely human with all the memories of my energy being locked in a man's form. This minute body I now possessed was as alien to me as it was possible to get. The thoughts, feelings and sheer physicality of the little animal almost blew my mind. I couldn't seem to control any of the legs and sight through the eyes of my host was an extraordinary dilemma. Everything looked so huge!

I flopped around on the hard concrete, spinning around in circles and feeling like a complete idiot. If I couldn't control an ant, how was I ever going to control another human being? Other ants rushed at me, pushing and probing. I was obviously giving some very unusual signals and I hoped the other ants weren't going to attack me. Fortunately, they tried to assist me, guiding me to my feet and ushering me over to the protection of a rock.

I didn't know what else to do or how to respond to them. They seemed to be making some high pitched clicking noises and moving their antennae in more and more agitated motions. I was becoming extremely apprehensive and feared they might see me as an interloper. Desperation rushed through me in a mighty torrent of adrenalin.

"How ironic would it be to survive the wormhole, only to be killed by an army of ants? That would be crazy", I decided. "Although, on reflection, it's probably what I deserve."

In my sixty years of life on Earth, how many of these little guys had I needlessly killed without a single thought? How many had I poisoned to keep them away from the inner sanctums of my house? How many of their homes had I blithely destroyed while digging in the garden?

My mind harkened back to a time when I had parked my campervan under a tree. Right outside the door, on the ground, was a green ant's nest. For no good reason other than that they were inconvenient to me, I started squashing hundreds of these ants into the ground. Within seconds, I had a number of the insects on my head and neck, biting me. I couldn't believe they had scurried up my body so quickly!

 I gazed upwards and realized that part of the colony had been gathering food in the tree and were jumping off the branches in response to what I was doing to their nest some eight feet below. I realised then that they had a high degree of communication as well as a frenzied desire to protect their fellow compatriots.

"You were a selfish and foolish man," I chided myself, self-loathing and guilt planting one more black mark on my heart. "Now it may be their turn for revenge if I don't work out a way to get out of this pickle."

I tried desperately to leap out of the little ant's body, but it was to no avail. I seemed to be trapped.

"Think Grant, think," I pressed.

I decided my only chance was to calm myself and try to stop giving off negative signals. I blocked my mind and started feeling the music from the Afterlife. It had an instantaneous calming effect and I started swaying to the beat.

The ants reacted also. Their movements slowed, they stopped chirping and started gently stroking me. It was as if these ants could feel the music through me. I, in turn, started to feel at one with the ants and was finally able to start controlling the little ant's body.

I began by slowly moving about and then once I gained confidence, tried climbing some twigs and rocks.

"This is so exciting," I thought as I scaled a small dead tree and walked upside down on the underside of one of the branches. "A scientist would sell his soul to swap places with me at the moment."

It was an amazing experience and one I would have loved to have continued longer, but time was of the essence. First though, I had to work out HOW to leave. I noticed a young cat slinking along the shadows of the nearest building and decided she or he would be my next target. I steadied my thoughts then willed myself into the cat.

In an instant I had achieved my objective. I hadn't even had time to say goodbye to my ant companions.

"Why couldn't I leave the ant's body like that when I tried before?" I wondered, and then the realisation dawned.

Niara's words echoed in my head, "You must relax and think yourself there."

I hadn't been able to relax. I had been too apprehensive about the intent of the ants. Fear had blocked my ability to transfer myself.

This time, it was only a matter of a few minutes before I had total control of the sinuous, feline form. I enjoyed the cat's lithe agility and revelled in the tightly coiled muscles which sprang into life as I climbed a rickety old fence to survey the dismal landscape. I jumped from the cat to a dog and lingered there a short while.

I could feel the anxiety and desperation the dog was experiencing. His owners had probably perished and he was left to fend for himself, alone and confused. My presence seemed to be comforting the dog as Niara had predicted.

Satisfied that I was now ready to inhabit a human, I left my canine companion and entered the research centre in pursuit of a kindly soul.

CHAPTER X

If I'd thought my task was going to be easy I was sadly mistaken. I'd never come across so many dour, brusque and stony people in all my life. I entered room after room, examining each and every person I encountered.

"This is unbelievable," I complained to the air, feeling more and more frustrated with every passing minute.

How was I going to be able to do anything without a body to inhabit? I continued my search, taking careful note of the laboratories and the positions of the guards. I figured wherever the guards were, the vaccine couldn't be too far away.

I kept on seeking but bitterness, anger and hostility blocked my every attempt to connect.

"What is wrong with these people?" I muttered peevishly.

I wondered how Niara and the others were getting on. If they were doing as well as me, the world was in real trouble. I was two thirds through an entire section and I still hadn't seen a glimmer of hope. Despair began to tentacle through me. I tried to shrug it off but even the air here seemed dank and malevolent.

My search brought me down into the bowels of the building and to my horror I discovered this was where the experimental laboratory animals were housed. Rats, mice, dogs, cats and monkeys were crammed into small cages in a dismal abyss of hopelessness. I didn't see Mikhail to begin with. He stood silent and still before a sealed glass compartment, one hand pressed against a pane. I peeped inside and if I'd had blood it would have run cold.

A small monkey lay within, spreadeagled on its back with its limbs tethered by metal manacles. Its body was blistered with the pus filled boils of smallpox and its eyes were dull and glazed with pain. Incisions covered its torso where different products had been inserted to monitor the effects of whatever medication was being trialled. The empathy which Mikhail felt for this anguished and mistreated primate was all encompassing. It permeated his body from top to toe. At last I had found one decent, loving person in this hateful place and I slipped quickly and easily into his body.

The takeover was as smooth as silk and I felt just as I imagined a pilot must feel on achieving a perfect touchdown. Once I'd settled inside, I quickly realised my dilemma. What would I be able to accomplish in the body of a laboratory assistant? I'd hoped to inhabit a top influential scientist, someone who could persuade the other scientists in the facility to work on the project the Guides would put in place. Who would take any notice of a lab technician?

"Still, beggars can't be choosers, as the old saying goes," I reminded myself grimly.

Hurrying from the dingy bleakness of the animal quarters, I tried calling Niara with all my might.

"Why hadn't I thought to arrange a meeting place or a way to get in touch?" I asked the air in frustration.

It wasn't like me to leave so many loose ends dangling.

"I've gotten into the habit of relying on Niara for everything and become lazy," I decided.

The sound of shoes treading briskly along the corridor alerted me to the presence of another and I quickly glanced up. A white haired man in a lab coat was striding briskly toward me so I hung my head subserviently and made to walk past him.

"Are you not speaking to me now Grant?" came Niara's sweet voice from the direction of the man who had stopped beside me.

Mikhail's mouth dropped open.

"Is that really you?" I managed to choke out, surprise almost numbing my new vocal chords.

"Yes Grant, it is really me. Do I make an agreeable man?" she laughed.

"Indubitably my dear, very distinguished indeed I must say!" and we both chuckled.

Laughter was like an antidote for all the adrenalin rushes of the past few hours and I was sure it helped Niara as much as me.

"Grant, we have been very blessed to find the scientist I now inhabit. He is a very senior doctor and commands great respect. It took a great deal of effort to possess his form. He was almost totally inured to goodness but luckily for us he still retained a chink for me to enter. Some of the other Guides have also found hosts so we must hurry to the vaults and collect some of the vaccine."

We quickened our pace and hastened to the appointed place.

"Here are our companions," Niara called as we turned a corner in the maze of corridors.

Standing before us were two people. One appeared to be a cook and the other a cleaner.

"Is this it? Is this all the Guides we have here? How on Earth are we going to convince the guards to let us enter the vaults or overpower them when there are only the four of us?"

"As I am sure you are well aware Grant, there is a dearth of suitable humans for us to occupy here. We will have to make do with the people we have occupied. I have created some paperwork which gives us permission to acquire some of the vaccine. We need to find some lab coats for Genady and Viktor. With any luck we will appear as a delegation of scientists working on a new project."

"I've got a bad feeling about this," I warned.

"Grant, if you have a better plan I am willing to listen."

It only took me a few seconds to realise that I was stumped.

"I'm sorry, Niara. No, I can't think of a damn thing which would work any better," I growled, frustration getting the better of me.

"Very well then, let us make our attempt. Follow me please gentlemen."

We continued on, stopping only to obtain the necessary accruements for the other two guides.

Mikhail's nerves quivered as we neared the entrance to the vault. Half a dozen very professional looking soldiers with semi-automatic weapons stood at the entrance. Niara swept forward, her host body looking cool and commanding.

"Here are our papers. Please permit entrance," she declared authoritatively as she handed her official looking documents to the soldier who appeared to be in charge.

He grunted as he took them insolently.

"This guy is no fool," I worried, trying hard not to let my concern show.

He was having none of it.

"You are denied permission to enter. Guards, arrest them!" he commanded, pointing his weapon directly at us.

Fear engulfed me and I turned my head in search of a way to flee but there was no escape and we were quickly surrounded.

"You two stay here," said the Captain as he pointed to two of the guards. "The rest of you come with me while we escort this lot to Sector seven."

I was mortified at the thought of being thwarted so quickly. I looked at Niara but her concerned expression gave me the distinct impression she hadn't come up with a plan 'B' yet. I wracked my brains as our footsteps echoed along the corridor.

"Think Grant, think, before it's too late," I commanded myself.

As we neared the end of the hallway, the hint of an idea began to surface.

"It probably won't work but we have to try something. If we fail now it will be ten times harder to get past those guards on a second attempt," I reasoned as I telepathically connected with Niara.

"Niara, I have a plan. Can you channel the music from the Afterlife so the guards can hear it?"

"Yes, of course," she replied curiously. "What do you have in mind Grant?"

"It's just something that worked with the ants. With a bit of luck it might work with these goons. Please hurry," I urged.

The music started and the guards slowed to a halt.

"What is that music? Where is it coming from?" interrogated the Captain. "I have never heard anything so beautiful in my life."

They stood there transfixed, mesmerised by the sounds filling the hallway. I could see their facial expressions begin to soften and their eyes began to glaze. I could feel the wall of hardness crumbling away from the Captain. Slowly but surely the goodness deep within him began to bubble to the surface. I waited for as long as I dare.

"Now is my chance!" and struck with the speed of a well-trained warrior.

I leapt from Mikhail into the Captain's body, forcing my way in and taking control while he was still mesmerised. As the music died down Niara connected with me telepathically.

"Excellent work Grant. I see you are not just a pretty face."

I laughed inwardly at her joke. This soldier I now inhabited had one of the ugliest faces you were ever likely to see on a human being.

"Turn around and take these men back to the laboratory. I have made a mistake. Their paperwork is in order," I commanded the guards.

"Are you sure Captain Tarasov? We are normally informed of incoming scientists," the second–in–command quizzed.

"You dare question me! I have given you an order. It is not up to you to think," I challenged, all the while keeping my fingers crossed that he didn't smell a rat.

"Yes Sir!" he responded automatically.

I grabbed Mikhail by the scruff of the neck and pushed him along in front of me as he was looking decidedly confused. Upon reaching the laboratory doors, I ordered the guards who had been left guarding the entrance to unlock the gateways.

"All you men will go about your duties while I escort the scientists to their destination. I will be staying with them until their experimentation is completed. This is a top secret mission so I advise you to keep your mouths shut or you will be answerable to me. IS THAT CLEAR!" I barked.

"YES SIR!" they all answered in unison.

We quickly disappeared into a labyrinth of hallways, down into the solid, cavernous interior of the vault. Niara located the precious samples and we headed to the laboratories. We managed to find a lab which was vacant and the Guides immediately set to work.

"What are you going to do Niara?" I asked inquisitively.

"Grant, are you aware of how smallpox vaccine is made?" she asked me.

"No, I wouldn't have a clue."

"The vaccine contains live vaccinia virus, a virus in the orthopoxvirus family and closely related to variola virus, the agent that causes smallpox. Pulp is scraped from vaccinia-infected animal skin, mainly calf or sheep, with phenol added to a concentration sufficient to kill bacteria but not so high as to inactivate the vaccinia virus. The vaccine is then freeze dried and sealed in ampoules for later re-suspension in a sterile buffer. Immunity results from inoculation under the skin with a bifurcated needle which causes multiple puncture sites," she informed me succinctly.

"That's interesting, but how are you going to alter the formula to kill the mutated blackpox strain?" I asked.

"Good question Grant. I believe this scientist I inhabit has the answer. We must convince him to help us. I am going to transfer myself to Mikhail so we can talk to him," Niara said as she left the doctor's body and entered Mikhail's in one smooth motion.

We gave the doctor a few minutes to recover as he was very disorientated and confused.

"Where am I? What's happening?" he moaned.

"You are in one of the laboratories Doctor Petrov and we need your help," Niara explained.

"What are you talking about? Help with what? Aren't you one of the lab technicians?" the doctor asked suspiciously.

"Yes doctor, I am," Niara confirmed. "You are aware that billions of people are dying from the blackpox strain, are you not?"

"Well, yes. I am not blind! It is tragic," he sniffed. "Why? Do you think you can help? You have not suddenly become a scientist or a medical practitioner have you?" the doctor inquired disparagingly.

Niara drew Mikhail's body up straight and proud.

"No Sir, but if I was I know I would not be allowing my fellow human beings to succumb to this cruel fate," Niara, through Mikhail, stated passionately.

"Doctor we know you have the completed formula for the vaccine. Please tell us before it is too late!" Niara beseeched.

A hint of fear crossed his face before a veil of secrecy came down.

"I don't know what you are talking about," he lied.

"Please Doctor! We have precious little time left. Help us."

"I have told you I can't help you. I don't know what you are talking about. Captain, could you please do your duty and take this insolent little rodent away? I'm busy enough as it is without these ridiculous interruptions," he said as he waved everyone away dismissively.

"THAT'S ENOUGH! You people only understand one form of persuasion," I interjected as I pressed the rifle barrel to his lips. "We don't have time for your antics or your lies. You have three seconds to start talking before I blow your head off. I'm sure you realise we don't really need you. We know you will have the formula hidden here somewhere. We'll find it eventually. ONE, TWO...."

"No! Please stop! Do not shoot! I will tell you," he begged, terror reducing him to a quivering shell of a man.

My bluff had worked. I had a gut feeling that the good Doctor was probably terrified of the ugly-faced Captain and would be easily intimidated by him.

"Okay, start talking," I ordered.

"The formula is in my office safe. We have a number of doses ready but they haven't been properly tested and I have strict instructions not to release any of the vaccines until I receive the order," he blubbered.

"Doctor, it may be too late by then. We cannot wait," cautioned Niara.

"You do not understand! I will be killed if I disobey orders," the doctor declared intensely.

"Listen doctor. There are worse things than dying," I said through Tarasov. "Living a life where you are responsible for one death is bad enough, let alone hundreds of millions or maybe even billions. This is bigger than all of us. Don't sit back in fear like some snivelling coward. It's time to make a stand and do what you know is right. Risking your life for the greater good is real living and something you won't regret in the long term. Look at me; I bet you never would have believed I would risk my life and career for the sake of saving others?

"No, I must admit you are correct in that assumption," the Doctor said shakily.

What do you say doctor? We need as much help as we can get," I implored, passion warming my words and impelling them into his almost frigid heart.

Doctor Petrov pondered for a moment then stood up.

"You are right. I am sick of living in fear and living with guilt. I will help you and enlist as many technicians as possible to start mass production.

I hope I have the heart and stomach for this but I feel I have no other choice… We will go and save the world!" Petrov announced, shrugging off his mantle of fear.

"Ours is not to reason why, ours is but to do or die," he declared, as he recalled the words from the Charge of the Light Brigade. "I should have been doing this a long time ago. I will make up for that error now. We require a test subject," the doctor declared imperiously.

The vision of the pitiful little monkey lying shackled in his glass containment cage popped into my mind.

"Mikhail's monkey!" I cried.

"Success with an animal may not mean success for a human but perhaps it is just as well to test the vaccine on a primate to begin with. Yes, we will try the monkey first," Petrov ordered.

After collecting the test vaccine, we marched back as a group with a mission to where the monkey was being held in the basement section.

Once there, the doctor injected the solution into the monkey's wasted flesh then carefully removed the manacles. Niara reached in, scooping the little one into Mikhail's arms. She cradled him like a baby and I had a brief glimpse of the lovely mother she might have been during her life on Earth.

"All we can do now is wait," she whispered as the monkey clung to what little life was left to it.

Hours passed and still the monkey lived on. My human form grew weary and wanted to sleep but I didn't dare let it. I wasn't about to risk letting Tarasov free.

"It should have been starting to work by now," Niara worried.

I tried to think of something to say to comfort her but nothing useful came to mind so I kept my mouth shut. As the sun broke on yet another scorching hot day, Niara offered the small creature some water and a little food. To our surprise and delight, the monkey took both then slept again. When he awoke an hour later, it was obvious he wanted more.

"Grant, I think we have our antidote!" Niara cried excitedly.

Within three hours we were sure of it. The little guy was a lot better. He had lost the glazed look from his eyes and was taking notice of the things around him. He even tried to stand up but was still too weak.

"You can try that again when you're a bit stronger kiddo," I said, stroking the matted fur on his gaunt little body.

"Grant, we must go and tell the others of our success. It is time to enlist the help of doctors around the world to produce as much of the vaccine as possible and inoculate the remaining population."

Niara found Doctor Petrov and asked him to explain what he did to enhance the effectiveness of the vaccine so she could pass the information on to the guides who were at the other smallpox facility, the C.D.C in Atlanta, U.S.A.

Doctor Petrov explained.

"Firstly I managed to synthesise the vaccine. After that process I encased the vaccine in fatty droplets called liposomes and then packaged the droplets together in concentric spheres and chemically welded them together to form nanoparticles. Once injected they degrade quickly, releasing the vaccine and triggering an excellent T cell response," he finished proudly.

Niara channelled the information through to the other Guides. Within twelve hours she had wonderful news.

"Grant, thousands of scientists have volunteered to help. There are ten other secret facilities around the world which have the smallpox virus and stocks of smallpox vaccine ready to be enhanced," she exclaimed excitedly. "There is a real chance of making a difference and more quickly than first thought."

From then on, everything was a whirl of activity. Vaccines were being produced at an unimaginable scale. Hundreds of thousands of guides were hosting bodies and working beside countless volunteers ensuring the vaccine was distributed to every person on the planet. Soon it became a waiting game to see if the first vaccinated areas would turn the tide of human misery. Would the vaccine work as well on humans as it did on Mikhail's little monkey?

Little by little the news started filtering back. After two days of vaccination some appeared to be recovering, though many more were still dying, apparently too far gone to be saved. After three days, the news appeared a little better but still too early to call. It wasn't until the fifth day that we knew the tide had definitely turned.

The relief and euphoria of realising we were starting to win the battle was overwhelming. To see the pride and joy exhibited on the faces of Guides and volunteers who had toiled away tirelessly together was something I will never forget. They knew they had done something exceptional and their lives would never be the same. The next day I went to see Doctor Petrov.

"How are you today doctor, after witnessing a miracle?" I inquired happily.

"Please Captain, call me Oleg," the good doctor implored. "And to answer your question, I believe this miracle has saved me along with the rest of the world. I will forever be grateful to you and Mikail for forcing my hand."

"I'm glad to hear you say that Oleg. Unfortunately, I have some news which may distress you."

Before he could ask what I meant, I held my hand up and continued.

"I haven't slept for seven days and I am going to lie down to sleep. When I eventually awaken I will not recall anything that has occurred since before we came to you demanding the formula. Sadly, the relationship I have built with you over this last week will cease to exist and I will go back to being the brutal person you have always known me as. You will also notice many of the other workers will suffer the same case of amnesia."

The doctor interrupted. "I don't understand what you are saying. What are you talking about?"

"I can't explain why this is going to happen. You will have to draw your own conclusions. What I can tell you is that it is imperative that you convince me of what we have achieved and that I was a willing participant. Make sure that I don't have access to any weapons and you have many others with you to corroborate your story. I will not be easily persuaded. My advice is to tell me that when we all heard the music we collectively decided to vaccinate the world and that I am suffering temporary amnesia through overwork. Do you understand Oleg?"

"No, I am afraid I do not comprehend at all. However I will prepare for this situation if it arises. It is a shame; I was really starting to like you," Oleg confessed.

"Yes it is a shame. However, no matter what happens in the future doctor, remember you are a hero. You have saved more lives than anyone else in history. You may or may not get recognised for it but you will know. Good luck Oleg, I hope we meet again."

With that I gave him a hug and walked away to one of the dormitories.

"Poor old Tarasov," I mused. "It's amazing I haven't killed him through lack of sleep. With a bit of luck he won't wake up for a couple of days. He certainly won't be pleasant to be around when he finds out what's been going on," I thought as I lay down on the bed. Tarasov fell asleep instantly as I slipped from his body and went looking for Niara.

Niara was still busy co-ordinating the Guides and volunteers for the remaining few areas to be vaccinated. Once finished she turned to me and said,

"I feel your presence Grant. You have divested yourself from Tarasov's body."

"Yes Niara. I thought I had better let him sleep before he went into a coma," I laughed.

"Niara, this has been an incredible experience for me. Thank you for allowing me to come with you."

"You have proven to be a valuable asset, Grant, and have been a welcome addition," Niara responded.

"Niara, I have been amazed that no guards or government officials have challenged us in this entire week. Surely someone has leaked information to the government on what we've been up to," I stated.

"Perhaps Grant. However, the comings and goings of a research facility are inconsequential compared to what has been happening on the planet. Even if the government knew, they might have been relieved that somebody was finally doing something," Niara concluded.

"You are probably right. So, what do we do now?"

"I need to get you back to your transition area Grant. The other Guides are in control now. We seem to be containing the smallpox epidemic so I see no reason to keep you here any longer."

"Could I ask one more favour of you Niara? Could I have one last look in Australia before we return? Something has been tugging at me for the last two days and I feel a desperate need to go back."

"Permission granted. Think of the area you desire the most and I will return with you," Niara instructed.

In a flash we were on the Sunshine Coast, south-east Queensland. As we surveyed the area, dismay and then utter horror warped the enjoyment of being home once more. This once beautiful and pristine area was a dust bowl. Where water had once flowed in abundance along the myriads of creeks, rivers and wetlands, long cracks now snaked their way in criss-cross patterns like a crazy mosaic.

Everything was withered and arid under the scorching heat of the sub-tropical sun. Death hung in the air like an oppressive dictator. As in Koltsovo, the bodies were piled high in the street and the same haunted expression hung on every face of the living.

"Niara," I thought despairingly. "Even if the smallpox epidemic has been brought under control, how are we ever going to make it rain?"

My question would have to remain unanswered for the time being. I felt compelled to head for the local hospital. The tugging feeling I had been experiencing in Russia was much stronger here. I decided to invade an intern's body and take a tour of the wards. I didn't know why. I just felt a desperate need to investigate.

Piteous sights met me at every bed. Bodies wracked with the dreaded disease lay in filth and squalor. There weren't enough able-bodied nurses to care for them all. Some of the patients had already died, quite a few days ago by the look and smell of things. Tormented moans filled the air.

"There is a cure. Just hold on for a little while longer," I fervently told each of the living.

I had no idea if they heard or were comforted but I felt the need to at least try and give them hope. Obviously this hospital had only recently acquired the vaccine.

Eventually, my wanderings brought me to a bed at the end of the last ward in the hospital. At first I thought the shrivelled old lady who lay there had already died, but on closer inspection I could see that she still breathed though her breaths were shallow and fast. I was strangely drawn to this poor, dying woman and I moved closer.

There was something familiar about the shape of her nose and the curve of her mouth. I glanced at the name tag above the bed and was fixated with shock. This was my baby Casey, my eldest daughter.

"NO! NO! NO!" I wailed, torrents of tears cascading down the intern's face.

I rushed to her side and threw my arms around her failing body and pushed my face close to hers.

"Daddy is here darling. Daddy is here! Don't die my sweetheart. Medicine is coming that will make you well. Oh please Casey, hang on!" I cried urgently, hugging her to me, intent on warming her cold, unresponsive body.

She didn't open her eyes. Instead, her breathing became ever fainter until eventually I couldn't discern a breath at all. My beloved little girl had died in my arms and I felt as if my heart had been ripped out of me. Gut-wrenching sobs erupted and I cried as I'd never cried before.

Because of my own early demise, I had never experienced the loss of someone inside my own immediate family. Even my mother was still alive at the time of my death. Whilst I had lost my father, we had been estranged for a long time. This was a completely new experience for me, raw and irrational.

I couldn't bear the pain and left the intern's body, beside myself with grief. It was then that I saw Casey looking down on her dead body. She turned towards me, recognising my presence and whispered "Daddy!" before she fell into her trance and her pale aura began its ascent to Nyame.

Suddenly it hit me. My girl would have to navigate the worm hole and it was still being blocked. There hadn't been time yet to slow the influx of essences.

"Niara, I need you!" I screamed in total anguish and instantly she was there.

"We have to save her! We have to save Casey!" I blubbered and raced to Casey's drifting side.

Niara had sized up the situation immediately and joined us.

"All right Grant. I will assist you. We must shelter your child through the worm hole. It will be difficult in the extreme but we will do what we can. It will be even more imperative that we get the timing right. Casey cannot help herself. If we align ourselves on each side of her perhaps we can shoulder her through," Niara exclaimed.

Far too soon we were in sight of the entrance to the worm hole.

"Niara, I don't think I can do this without you but I hate the thought of you risking your life for me and my daughter. I want to release you from any obligation you may feel to assist me. There is more important work for you to do transitioning all these souls," I said, finally realising what a valuable piece of this Afterlife puzzle she actually was.

"Grant hush now. Every life is important. You and your daughter are my responsibility. I told you before we left that you must never leave my side. I am not about to abandon you now. Let us concentrate on saving your daughter and ourselves. Hopefully, through the grace of Nyame, we will come out the other side alive."

Life energies were flowing around us thick and fast now. Between the two of us, we bumped and steered Casey through to the freest flowing areas. The blinding flashes and crackling noises of the obliterated ones were unnerving me.

"Grant, all will be well!" I heard Niara say, and her words of confidence strengthened me.

With renewed resolve, I focused on getting us through. We floated closer, bumping Casey in an effort to restrain her from being drawn in prematurely. The forces which were being placed on Casey to move her on to the Afterlife were more than Niara's and mine combined energies. We both shifted in front of Casey, pushing back as hard as we could, trying desperately to slow her momentum so we could time our run precisely.

Casey slowed, but even giving it everything we had, I could still feel us being forced ever closer to the entrance.

"PUSH NIARA. PUSH HARD," I kept on urging.

Our energies were being tortured in the effort to stop Casey. Horribly, it was all to no avail. We were being forced into the narrowing centre like leaves in a whirlpool. I had one last look backwards and saw how close we were to imminent death.

"This is it, we're goners," I thought. "Well, at least I died trying to save you," was my final consolation as I clung to Casey, waiting for the inevitable.

Suddenly we stopped. Incredibly, the entrance blocked in the final seconds. We now found ourselves being pushed in the opposite direction as the trapped Auras swelled in response to the heat and friction.

BOOM! The explosion flung us backwards and I was dazed and disorientated.

Through all the noise and confusion I heard Niara's forceful command, "GO!"

Like a switch being thrown, I reacted immediately. Moving as fast as we could, we pushed and shoved and shouldered our way through the throng. The tension was electrifying, and for one awful second I almost lost contact with Casey, but eventually we forced our way through to comparative safety.

"Hurry Grant!" Niara telegraphed to me. "You must keep moving. Do not get pulled back into the next explosion."

Within seconds, a further blast was triggered but we were safely beyond the limits of its force. Once we were clear, a feeling of excitement, coupled with euphoria, overwhelmed me.

"We made it Niara! Can you believe it, we made it through alive!"

"Yes we did Grant. That was a close call but together we succeeded."

"Thank you for being there for me Niara. I will never forget the debt I owe you," I promised.

"There is no debt Grant. I told you in the beginning, I was here to help you find your way and that also includes your daughter, so think no more of it."

As we neared the Afterlife end of the wormhole, Niara softly said, "It is time to let Casey go now Grant."

"What are you talking about? I can't let her go. I've just found her. I can help her," I yelled, mortified at the thought of losing Casey again. "Niara, you know I'd do anything for you, but don't make me do this, I beg you."

"Grant, each one of us has our own path to travel. You cannot travel Casey's path any more than she can travel yours. She must go through the transitions alone. Take comfort in the thought that you have enabled her to have the gift of becoming a Being. Perhaps one day you will meet again? But for now you must let her go," Niara instructed.

I moved away from Casey and she continued on her way.

"Goodbye darling, keep safe," I whispered and watched until she had disappeared from my view, not knowing if I would ever see her again.

A horrible feeling of aloneness swamped me, but fortunately it only lasted a short while. I was soon returned safe and sound to the transitions and all negative feeling was quickly nullified. Instead, I began to see the positives of what Niara had said.

"I sure hope we'll meet again one day. Maybe I'll see not only Casey, but Laura, Chase and Skye. What a reunion that will be," I reflected as Niara appeared before me.

"Grant, I have just had word of events on Earth. The vaccination program is progressing well. The death rates are dropping rapidly. And Grant, I have saved the best news for last... It has started to rain!"

CHAPTER XI

"How are you feeling Grant?" Niara questioned me on her third visit after our traumatic adventures on Earth.

"I'm great, Niara," I responded cheerfully. "In fact, things are a bit too quiet around here after our recent sojourn."

"Then I think it is time for you to leave here and move to the next stage of your transition. We will go to another area where there are objects, lights and many others like us for you to meet."

"That should be interesting. When will we be leaving?"

"Would you like to go now? I can implant the image of where you must go if that is your preference."

"Onwards and upwards. That is definitely my preference," I replied and immediately saw a place of brightness and strangeness within my mind's eye.

Using my knowledge of projection, I allowed myself to flow into this new world. It was easier than walking through a doorway and I couldn't help a little surge of pride at my hard won ability. Niara was beside me in an instant.

"Observe your surroundings Grant and then absorb them," were her first words to me.

And yes, there certainly was plenty to absorb. There appeared to be millions of Niara's and my ilk everywhere, in every colour, shade and hue, twinkling and flashing in more abundance than any starry night I'd ever seen. A vast array of ghostly forms and rainbows met my enchanted eyes. The light here was soft and gentle, almost comparable to the light at twilight, but clearer and infinitely nicer.

The music was here also, playing softly in the background, almost creating a world of its own. It was like every pleasurable sound I've ever experienced all rolled into one. The thunder of waves breaking on the shore, the wind whispering through a forest, the sweetness of birdsong, the passion of an orchestra playing a beautiful piece of music and the delight one hears in a baby's giggle. I wished I could explain it to myself better, but it was beyond me. Every time I heard that music it seemed like a new experience.

Intriguing smells assailed me. My mind flitted trying to identify them, but it was impossible. Again, there were fleeting references to things I knew, like freshly mown grass, perfume and the glorious scent of Daphne. Onions cooking on a barbecue, the kids when they'd just hopped out of the bath, fresh air in the mountains. Those smells were there but they weren't. It was a glorious medley of aromas, indescribably delicate and delightful.

There were objects something like flowers and trees, but in reality, were nothing like anything on Earth. They appeared almost as if made of shimmering liquid in shades of gold, silver, copper and bronze. Swirling, moving, pulsing with life, they held no particular shape but constantly changed to the symphony of sounds.

The fascinating designs seemed to replicate the feelings I received from the music. Starting from a beautiful field and then bursting into thousands of butterflies, before merging back into a snow-capped mountain. Sometimes the colours would trickle into one another, only to spray outwards in an endless kaleidoscope of imagery. Other times, one colour would appear dominant, almost solid, before melting away to near translucence before being re-joined by its colour partners. Here was a world infinitely more beautiful than anyone could ever imagine.

"This is unbelievable," was all I could say to Niara. "If I'd known this was here, I would have been chafing at the bit to get out of where I was learning to move, and yet I was happy there until now."

"That would be understandable," Niara empathised. "But where you were was necessary for you to be introspective, to begin the healing process and to learn how to shift. The delight you experience here would have made your learning more complicated and difficult."

"So is this where I'll be staying from now on?" I asked distractedly, still trying to absorb the pureness of this place.

"You will be here for a time," Niara said. "Again, it will depend on yourself as to how long you remain. As before, there are processes that you must attend to before you attain your purpose."

"When will my lessons start?"

"They have already started Grant."

I didn't see how they could have, but I wasn't going to argue. I was enjoying myself too much and for once I couldn't even be bothered with a question. I don't know how long we stayed, watching the wondrous sights before us. Everything was so fascinating, time seemed to stand still. Eventually though, Niara grabbed my attention by suggesting an introduction to the other Beings. As soon as she felt my affirmation, we connected with the closest Aura to us.

How unreal yet wonderful that first conversation was with another Light Being. There was no awkwardness; it was as if we were communicating on a completely different plateau. Total acceptance from the Aura before us enveloped me.

"If given the chance, how could I ever go back to Earth and leave this?" I wondered.

I had never felt or witnessed such unconditional relating in my life. Oh, I'd believed I had, but it was a pale shadow in comparison. The closest I'd ever experienced to this on Earth was when my children were very young. I'd come home from work and they would race out to greet and cuddle me as if I had been gone a year. It was that same unconditional love I was now experiencing, yet seemingly on a higher level.

If I'd thought the first aura I met was the only one I would connect to in this way I was wrong, for it wasn't too long before I was pleasantly surprised to find this marvellous form of association applied to every Aura we came in contact with. It appeared that there were zero signs of animosity, judgement or aloofness anywhere in this fabulous place. Everywhere we went I was greeted with love and happiness.

The feelings that I felt from this form of love and honour were a wonder to me. They poured through me like soothing balm, binding wounds I wasn't even aware I had. They were the calamine lotion on the itches and scratches of my former life, the blue bag which took the pain from the stings and endless barbs of wounding words and painful experiences. I'd had no idea what an open sore I still was.

There were so many things I had endured and buried away. That had been my method of self-protection. Now I realised, all I'd been doing was burying my head in the sand, just like the proverbial ostrich. For the first time, a glimmer of understanding of what Niara was trying to achieve entered my thoughts.

In my former life on Earth, I'd found many people bottled their emotions because there were so many things which a person had no control over. Like the abusive speech of someone you cared for who could slice your heart into a thousand pieces. Or the cruel loss of a loved one, never being able to apologise to them for a wrong doing. None of those things could be revoked once they'd occurred. There was nothing to do but hide the pain away in the deepest recesses of your being.

Of course there were other things people attempted in an effort to alleviate their distress. Prayer was one of them. I had attempted to understand people praying. To me it was like voicing your concerns out loud. Once expressed, some problems become clearer and you could find a solution. Almost like writing things down in a brainstorming exercise. It's just that some people are auditory learners while others are visual or sensory learners.

What had amazed me though was when people would pray for seemingly irrelevant things. For instance, I've heard people pray for a water fountain to work or to have their golf club found. Couldn't they see how ridiculous it must be, to ask God to bother fixing something as obscure as a water fountain or finding a golf club? I didn't think they needed a miracle when a plumber could do the job just as well, and if you lost a golf club, there were plenty more still for sale.

One thing I did find disturbing was when, during a catastrophe, someone survived while others died. Certain people would tout the miracle of the person saved as an act of God singling that person out, without considering how painful this may be to the relatives of the people who perished. Those family members may then have decided that God didn't deem them or their loved one worthy of saving. I understand now it doesn't matter either way, but people on Earth certainly couldn't have known for sure. Further to that, Niara had explained miracles are only laws we don't understand.

"Perhaps I'm completely wrong about all of this as well?" I pondered. "I really do have a lot to learn."

I'd like to find out about supernatural occurrences. Not that I necessarily believed in them, but I'd known plenty of people who had. I knew a woman who was heavily into séances, tarot cards, clairvoyants and anything else that had a psychic bent to it. She firmly believed in guardian angels and foreseeing the future. She and many others were convinced they had seen or heard ghosts.

I'd always believed most things could be explained by natural occurrences. They say poltergeists are usually linked to a troubled, pubescent teenager and that it's the teenager who manifests all the weird things. However, there are many things that are very hard to explain, like channelling, where somebody could start talking or writing in an ancient language they had never studied, or someone prophesising a future event. There have been many cases where people have described an event in great detail, only for it to happen exactly as they described.

Edgar Cayce was a prime example. An American psychic, born in 1877 and a devout Christian, he appeared to have the ability to channel answers to questions and to diagnose people who were ill whilst he was in a hypnotic trance. Cayce would also predict future events and correctly foretold the First and Second World Wars, the Independence of India, the stock market crash of 1929 and the creation of the state of Israel. He was so successful, that more than three hundred books have been written about him. An organisation, the Association for Research and Enlightenment, was set up in his honour.

According to Edgar, his gifts became apparent when he was seven or eight, after he was visited by a bright vision of a winged figure, clothed in white, while sitting in a clearing reading the Bible. The vision asked the young boy what he wanted to do in life, to which Cayce responded "That he wanted to help people."

The following day, Edgar was having problems with his spelling homework. In his head, he heard the voice of the vision telling him to go to sleep so he could be helped. Obediently, he did as he was directed and fell asleep with his head on his spelling book. On awakening, he was able to spell every word.

After a period of forty-three years, giving fourteen thousand, eight hundred and seventy-nine readings for over six thousand people with astounding results, he was asked to explain the secret of his abilities.

"Apparently," he said, "I am one of the few who can lay aside their own personalities sufficiently to allow their souls to make this attunement to a universal source of knowledge...but I say this without any desire to brag. In fact I do not claim to possess anything that other individuals do not inherently possess. Truly, I do not believe there is a single individual who does not possess this same ability I have. I am certain that all human beings have much greater powers than they are ever conscious of...if they would only be willing to pay the price of detachment from self-interest."

I wanted to find out if astral planing was real or if there was any basis in astrology. I suddenly realised I was slipping back to my old habits of never-ending questions, the one thing which was probably going to stop me from ever attaining inner peace.

"Niara's right, I am a slow learner, but it's just so hard not to desire all this knowledge surrounding me. I will try to curtail myself, although I'm sure it wouldn't hurt to get one or two questions answered in the time that I'm here."

In the meantime, Niara and I spent joyous amounts of time communicating with a multitude of wonderful Beings. Sometimes we conversed with single Auras and at other times we congregated together in groups. It soon became apparent in our conversations that Niara and I had become minor celebrities.

There was still a lot of interest regarding the smallpox epidemic on Earth and the subsequent rescue of humankind. The place was buzzing with talk about how Niara had allowed a novice, who hadn't even left the void yet, to accompany her back to Earth and then amazingly, the novice had actually been helpful in saving the world. I didn't let on to any of the Auras it was me they were talking about.

I was having a great time, but I couldn't help wondering exactly what we were doing if these were meant to be lessons for me. Curiosity eventually overwhelmed my 'just having a good time' attitude, but before I could pop the question out of my head, Niara was already answering.

"Grant, we are waiting for the perfect connection."

"The perfect connection to what?"

"The perfect connection for you to meet. Somewhere here is an Aura that you will link with for the next stage of your transition."

"But you're my Guide, aren't you?"

I hadn't realised until now how much I'd come to rely on Niara's help and guidance.

"Yes Grant and I will be nearby, but this Being is the one who will help you release the emotional baggage which you have brought with you from your previous existence. All people have acquired problems that they must confront and deal with before they may move on. You will be helped, much in the same way as a psychologist might do on Earth, but with greater beneficial results."

"How will we know this Being?"

"I will not know, but you will."

"How will I know?"

"Grant, do you recall the moment when you made the shift that allowed you to project yourself? The link is similar. You will feel a profound drawing within you, just as two magnets join together once they are in close proximity."

I wasn't sure I liked the sound of that but I trusted Niara absolutely. If this is what I needed, then I'd do it.

"Why didn't you tell me that's what we were doing while we were meeting up with all these other Beings?"

"Because now you will be looking and waiting for the link instead of just enjoying the fellowship as you have been doing."

And she was right. From then on, every time I engaged with someone, I waited in anticipation for this link thing. I was so busy concentrating on it, that sometimes I'd miss the opening parts of the conversations completely.

"Now I wish you hadn't told me," I complained.

"Grant, you are trying too hard. Be peaceful and patient and it will happen."

Before, when I'd been trying to learn to move, Niara had been at me to push myself to the greatest degree. Now I had to do the very opposite.

"I wish she'd make up her mind," I grumbled.

It made me feel better to blame someone else for a bit. It took my mind off the link. Time passed. It was lovely here and I started to forget about connecting. I should have known that's when it would happen. The force hit me like a ton of bricks.

"It's this Being!" I yelled to Niara exultantly and linked with Kai in a mind-blowing explosion.

Understanding passed between us and I 'knew' Kai as he 'knew' me, as intimately as if we had been friends for decades. I felt his character traits. I acknowledged his goodness. I perceived without doubt his ability to assist me. At last the lessons would begin in earnest.

CHAPTER XII

"Relax Grant. Let your memories flow from you like a river," Kai encouraged.

"I've tried but I've run out of water," I retorted. "We've been at this for ages and I, for one, am pretty sick of it."

"Well Grant, this will only take as long as you need to release what is inside you. I had hoped we would be finished in less than a thousand years, but the way you're going, I'd better settle in for the long haul," he laughed.

That was Kai for you. Nothing seemed to faze him. Calm and cool as a cucumber.

The problem was, I didn't want my memories to flow from me. I didn't see the point in dredging things up from the past which I had blocked from my consciousness years and years ago. I truly couldn't remember what it was I was supposed to remember. I'd wracked my brain endlessly and nothing was coming to the forefront. I knew there was something, but for the life of me, I couldn't bring it to mind even if I'd wanted to. Kai was persistent though, I had to give him that. He was at me again.

"Grant, everything worthwhile requires effort. No-one will give you what you need on a silver platter. It is entirely up to you when this will happen but happen it must. You will have to summon your courage and face your fears. There is no other way. We believed you had gleaned the knowledge of participation for transition when you entered this space from your movement and meditation space. You are being cowardly," Kai stated quite calmly.

"I can't believe you would say that! I've always made a point of facing my fears. It was almost my mantra to my kids. No-one could ever accuse me of not facing my fears!" I spluttered. "I had a fear of heights so I forced myself to scale mountains, bungee jump off bridges and parachute out of planes. I made sure that my children clambered up fire tower ladders and slipped down the highest waterslides just about as soon as they could walk. I've thrown myself into the path of danger plenty of time just so I could conquer my fears. No-one has ever accused me of being a coward before."

"Then why are you inhibiting your memories Grant?"

"But I've told you I'm not. I can't remember any more than what I've already said. I've told you everything I can, warts and all."

"I wish this were true for your sake Grant, but we both know that's not the case. I want to help you but I can only do so when you are ready to help yourself. Why don't we attack the problem through your imagination? Perhaps that way you can divorce yourself from the immediate impact," Kai suggested.

"Okay," I sighed. "Why is every lesson so hard for me?"

"I think I can answer part of that question Grant. One of the reasons is because you were an atheist. The other is because you have spent much of your time in the Afterlife trying to discover why you didn't realise Nyame or this place existed when you were alive. It is incredibly hard for you to deal with circumstances you find illogical. You have never learnt to trust your feelings, to cast your fate into the hands of an unknown superior. You have trouble being submissive. When were you ever in a position where you were required to humble yourself? Unfortunately Grant, your lessons may not come easy. Believers often have less difficulty with the transitions."

"Great, that's just what I need, another long struggle."

Niara had said very much the same thing but in different words when I'd been trying to learn how to move. How do I learn to have faith in things I've never believed in? I was being challenged in so many ways. Nothing on Earth had or could prepare me for the tasks that were now before me. I didn't want to be resistant. I liked Kai and needed Niara. I knew they were there to help me. At the end of the day, it was up to me to develop myself.

"What do you suggest I try Kai?"

"Hallelujah," Kai laughed. "The man is finally going to REALLY try. I'm sure I can feel it in my bones, if you'll pardon the expression. So let's get down to business before you change your mind.

"I know this might sound a bit effeminate, but try to imagine yourself as a rosebud. As the sun shines upon you, open your petals slowly, layer by layer, to the life giving warmth. Feel yourself unfolding, gently but inexorably, exposing your inner essence to the vagaries of life.

"Allow the sunlight to penetrate deeper and deeper inside you, right to your very core. Feel everything that it is possible to feel and explore every nook and cranny in totality with no fear or regret. Trust fully in your subconscious search and what your existence offers... Now give yourself up to the euphoric feelings of Nyame," Kai advised.

With this wonderful picture implanted in my head, I endeavoured to obey. I saw myself as a young bud, healthy, strong and yearning to flower. Carried by the tide of instinct; in perpetuity I found myself opening to the world of my inner sanctum, my most vulnerable self. I relaxed, believing the centre of my being would not be violated. I welcomed the visitation of the presence's which would enable me to seed with other individuals. I unfurled and blossomed in an outpouring of certainty and conviction. What was before me was imperative for my continued bond with the energy of subsistence.

The release was incredible. I had never realised the weight I had carried. It was as if rocks were lifted from me and I floated into the air, lighter than an exhaled breath. Exhilaration shot through me, an amazing and electrifying jolt of extreme happiness. And then the terror set in. My life flooded before me.

There was nowhere to hide, no shelter from the events that I had concealed for so long. Shock, horror, terror, fear, revulsion, ripped through me like a knife through a chunk of meat. I recoiled like a rabid animal, crazed in my attempts to escape the self-loathing which encompassed me.

"Ride with it," I heard Kai say. "Know yourself, accept yourself and believe that everything has a reason for being."

It was the voice of sanity, the only thing which kept me from hurtling into the abyss of madness. I had no idea how long the chaos of my mind continued. When I questioned Kai about the length of time I'd been trapped in my dread of remembrance he said,

"It doesn't matter. All that's important now is you resolve what needs to be resolved and find your way through the labyrinth of worries which have encompassed your former path."

I was a different person. I no longer recognised the person I once was.

"Start with your earliest memory," Kai commanded.

"That's so long ago," I complained. "I seem to remember when I was no older than eighteen months, perhaps younger, being supine in a pram, fascinated by the ceiling fans at a Coles department store. I couldn't seem to tear my eyes from their circular motion."

"That's good," Kai encouraged. "Now how about the happiest memory you can think of as a child?"

"That one's easy Kai," I said a little more cheerfully. "My grandparents bought me a set of zoo animals for Christmas. I was only five or six years old and I knew they were very expensive because when I saw them in the shops, my mother told me she could never afford to buy me something so costly. I never believed it would be possible to receive a gift like that. When I tore off the wrapping paper I couldn't stop kissing the box. It was probably the only time I can recall when I was so excited and happy that I felt like crying."

"What about as an adult?"

"That's another easy one. It was the time I was travelling around Australia after Steve and I had parted and before I met Laura. I was completely on my own and didn't have to compromise with anyone. I'd travel, stop for a long lunch and read, do a little more travelling in the afternoon, then find a campsite and meet new people. I was under no pressure and could focus completely and selfishly on my own desires. I was so happy I wanted to burst into song the whole time.

"I thought I'd been happy back home in Canberra. I'd achieved such a lot in a short space of time. By most peoples' reckoning, I'd managed to overcome the obstacles of poverty and limited education to make quite a success of myself. I had a strong relationship going with a woman and I firmly believed I was on the right track for financial, physical and emotional security. None of the joy I felt at home compared with that little window in time when I didn't have to be anywhere, do anything, or consider anyone else's needs," I told Kai wistfully.

"Right," Kai said thoughtfully. "I need to know what your saddest memory was when you were a young boy."

My unease returned.

"Can't we just stick with the pleasant thoughts?"

"That is like asking for the day without the night or the sun without the moon," Kai explained. "Please continue."

"Well, my saddest memory as a child is when I was four or five years old and I threw a ball for a young Labrador we had at the time. As she ran to fetch it, she caught her side on the bumper bar of an old car that Dad had stored in the backyard for spare parts. A great flap of skin peeled back and the dog screamed in horrible pain. We took the dog to the vet where they cut this huge flap off as they couldn't stretch the skin enough to stitch it.

"Mum spent day after day smothering this enormous expanse of raw flesh with Mercurochrome, a type of disinfectant. It took weeks of nursing before Lady's wound healed. I was shattered at being responsible for the dog's suffering," I told him, shivering at the thoughts of the past.

"No, wait Kai!" I suddenly called out.

"I've just remembered my very saddest childhood memory. It was when my dog, Red, was killed on my eleventh birthday. He'd jumped the fence to chase after a female dog in heat. They were together on the road which ran alongside our house. A truck driver deliberately swerved to run him over. The other dog was able to get out of the way, but not Red. I was still mourning and crying over his death whenever I found myself alone, up to the age of fourteen," I told him, my voice cracking.

"And as an adult?"

This was getting harder and harder now. I remembered what it felt like to get a lump in your throat when emotions rose and made it difficult for speech. I sort of felt like that now.

"It was the day my dog Warra, one of my best friends, was put down. I was too distraught to take him to the vet myself so Laura took him. It should have been me who was with him at the end. I let him down in his hour of need. He deserved better. You were right, I am a coward."

My grief was almost palpable between Kai and I. Torrents of tears flowed through my mind.

"Okay, we're getting somewhere now," Kai said gently, breaking the spell of my remembered bereavement.

"Grant, has it ever struck you that animals seem to come before humans in your estimations?"

I'd never thought about it before, but I could see he had a point. Was I afraid to love people and accept their love in the same way that I could with a dog? Or was it that I didn't trust people enough to know if their love was genuine? Perhaps it was simply because I'd never suffered the loss of a person who was closer to me than some of my dogs, who were treated like family members?

The love I received from the dogs always seemed to be unconditional, no matter what I did or how old the dog became. You could rely on their consistency. Compared to that, my children, who have always loved me, could turn on me in the blink of an eye if I did something bad enough in their viewpoint. When the children were little, they spoiled me by being so genuinely excited to see me after any absence. As they got older, they stopped rushing to the door and eventually arrived at the stage of barely acknowledging me at all. Dogs are always there to greet you, even if they are so old they can barely walk. Before I could explore the thought any further, Kai continued his line of questioning.

"What made you the angriest you can ever remember in your younger days?"

"Mmm, that was when we kids were stuck in a car for hours, waiting for our parents to finish whatever they were doing at a pub or club, every once in awhile. The longest period I can remember being left was from four in the afternoon to midnight. We were so cold; we covered ourselves with some sacks to keep warm. Keira, Richard and I would practise swearing at them, something we would have had our heads knocked off for if they'd ever caught us. We kids thought we were really hard done by, even if Mum would pop out every so often and buy us an ice-cream."

"Another time was when I was about eleven. Richard was eighteen months older than me and a lot bigger. We'd had a fight and he was chasing me around the table to bash me up. He couldn't catch me so my father tripped me as I was running to allow Richard to give me a hiding. I was so incensed at the injustice of it all. It was bad enough having a father that wouldn't protect me from someone who was far heavier and stronger than me, let alone actually helping him to inflict pain on me. At the time I was so angry that I'd dream of the opportunity of smashing my father in the face like he'd allowed Richard to do to me."

"And when you were older?" Kai pressed.

This one was an absolute no-brainer.

"My angriest adult memory, one hundred percent, belongs to the occasion when Laura and I had to deal with those two drunken idiots on our Yellow Waters fishing trip."

Even thinking about it now made my blood curdle.

"Now I need to know the time you felt the most loved as a child."

My mind drifted back and once more I felt the unconditional love given to me by small children and a number of dogs. Here was that thought again and I delved deeper. Adults rarely gave that sort of love, and I have to say, I probably wouldn't enjoy it even if they did. To me it would seem too much like doting. I'd gone out with a girl who was a bit like that in my younger days and I hated her adoration and submissiveness. I ended up treating her like a doormat, something I wasn't proud of even at the time.

Shaking myself from my reverie, I responded to Kai's question.

"I guess it was when Mum would play games with me. It made me feel special and valued and I knew she must love me to find the time from her never ending grind of work and worries to spend quality, one on one time with me. She never missed tucking me into bed at the end of the day, hugging and kissing me and maybe tickling me to get a few giggles before sleep came," I recalled.

"What about being unloved?" Kai said and I could feel his interest heighten.

"I was about ten when my father developed the habit of greeting me with "Gidday Shithead," a grin on his face every time he saw me. He knew I loathed it, but I was powerless to stop him and he took great pleasure in that. He couldn't have made me feel more unloved if he tried and I hated him for making me feel worthless. Besides that, I always felt he favoured Keira over Richard and me.

"He was such a tyrant, especially when he was drunk. I was very frightened of my father even though he only hit me with his open hand or a belt. It was just that he was so unpredictable and powerful. Mum, on the other hand, would make us kids pick a willow switch from our tree and hand it to her to whip us with it if we did anything wrong. As we got older, the weapons progressed to the cane end of the feather duster, to a doubled over electric jug cord through to a riding crop.

"I'll never forget the last time Mum used that riding crop on us. Things had settled down and Mum was calm once again after having administered her justice on us. Keira bravely mentioned how painful the crop was and how we wished she wouldn't use it. Mum didn't believe the riding crop was painful enough to cause us undue distress, so she ordered Keira to hit her with it. The dismay on Keira's face was reflected on both Richard's face and mine. Talk about being caught between the devil and the deep blue sea."

"No Mum," Keira gasped.

"She knew as well as we did that if she hurt Mum it could go very badly for her. Mum had quite a temper. If she didn't do it however, the beltings from the crop would continue. Mum's next words clinched it."

"Hit me as hard as you can or I'll hit you with it!" she ordered.

"Keira did as she was told and brought the crop down with a heavy whack on Mum's back. The crop was never used again.

"Thinking back, my fear and anger nearly cost Dad his life. I was in the backyard chopping wood one day when I was about fourteen years old. Mum and Dad began arguing on the back step and Dad was rubbing the blade of a blunt knife across the back of Mum's neck. Within seconds, I was faced with the decision of whether to kill him or not. I knew I wouldn't warn him because I would only have one chance to complete the task. If I failed, I knew he would most likely take the axe and use it on me.

"To this day, I believe there were only two things which saved him. One was the bluntness of the knife. If he'd been holding a sharp knife, I would have had to act immediately and wouldn't have had time to evaluate the situation. Secondly, Mum glanced in my direction and locked eyes with me. With a mother's intuition, she guessed what I was contemplating and ceased the goading that had so inflamed her husband, and by doing so averted a certain tragedy," I trailed off, after re-living the forgotten memory.

"I will make no judgements but we are now at the centre of your flower Grant," Kai solemnly declared. "You must disclose the memory which really haunts you."

"I can't, Kai, I mustn't," I whimpered, startled by his statement. "How do you know there is a memory that haunts me? I can't possibly talk to you about it. No, I won't do it! I truly cannot."

"On the contrary, Grant. You must tell me. I will help you. Let's take it step by step from the beginning. How old were you?"

"Fifteen," I whispered.

"And whereabouts were you?"

"Working on a cattle and goat farm south-east of Canberra," I replied nervously.

I could feel my anxiety levels rising with each question.

"What did you do on the farm?"

"Just the usual farmhand chores. I rode horses, herding cattle and goats from one pasture to the next."

"Was there any other activity you were involved with?"

"The farmer taught me how to use a rifle and then asked me to go out and shoot any foxes or rabbits I saw… Kai, I don't want to do this anymore," I pleaded with him.

"Grant, be strong. With every word you speak you are releasing the toxin that has poisoned your mind and body all these years. Why do you think you had a cardiac arrest at such a relatively young age? The black sludge of your most buried memories devastated your heart, coating it with the slime of bitter regret and despair," Kai declared forcefully.

"All right, I'll try. I only went out shooting once. I didn't really want to kill animals but the farmer made it seem like it was something I should do, part of the job. I was just mucking around taking pot shots at rabbits. I was so far away that I reckoned they'd be pretty unlucky for me to actually hit one. And it was fun having a go at shooting the rifle.

"Late that afternoon I came across a fox stalking a rabbit and I stood still, deliberating which one to go for. I decided to go for the fox and sighted along the rifle barrel. Both animals were about two hundred and fifty feet away when I fired. It was a great relief when I realised I'd missed my quarry," I managed to choke out.

"Go on," Kai encouraged.

"You know, don't you Kai? Oh my God you know!" I sobbed. "I didn't mean it. It was an accident. I would have given anything for it not to happen. Please forgive me!"

"Talk Grant! Talk!" Kai commanded. "You mustn't stop now. Hold nothing back."

The words vomited from me in a rush of foulness.

"I'd taken the shot and the fox had run away but I thought I heard a sound. I went over to investigate. When I reached the spot, I saw blood on the ground, seeping from under some bushes. I pulled back the bushes and there was blood everywhere. Kai, I can't do this! I can't go on!" I wept.

"Tell me everything," Kai insisted.

Almost incoherently, I kept going.

"There.... there was a girl. She was covered in blood. Oh no, no, no! I'd shot her. I didn't know she was there. I'd shot her in the neck and she was dead. She had a huge wound to her neck and her eyes were wide open and staring. She'd bled to death in the time it had taken me to walk the two hundred and fifty feet.

"I didn't know what to do! I was only fifteen. Who would believe it was an accident? The police would never believe me. I'd be taken away from my family. I panicked. I ran and ran and I kept on running all the way back to the farmhouse. When I saw the farmer, I told him I didn't want to hunt animals anymore and I wanted to go home. He tried to convince me to stay the night but I was adamant. Either he took me home now or I'd walk the forty miles to town by myself.

"He took me home that night and I never went back. I never told anyone. Later, I read about her in the paper. The police were looking for her. She was a twelve year old who had run away from a nearby property. The story said she'd been hanging around with a bad crowd and probably ended up in Sydney. They never found her and I lived with this terrible secret the rest of my life, living a lie, never daring to tell a soul.

"At times the guilt was unbearable. I thought of killing myself a number of times but I never had the courage to go through with it. After a long time I just locked it up inside of me and tried to block it out. Sometimes, I'd almost convince myself that it had never happened, that I'd dreamt it. Then a missing child report would come out and all the memories would come flooding back.

"I felt so sorry for her parents but I was paralysed with fear. Confused and tormented, I procrastinated, not knowing where to turn, what to say, what to do? I left it too late to do anything. As months, then years passed, I convinced myself the longer I didn't tell anyone; the more likely it was that everyone would believe I'd murdered her on purpose. I couldn't even let her parents know anonymously where their daughter was for fear of the police working out that I'd been there and tracking me down.

"I was caught in my own nightmare. The only thing I could think of was to trap the memory in the toolbox of my mind and padlock it away forever. I've tried to live a good and decent life ever since. You're the first person I've ever told Kai. Do you believe me? Do you believe it was an accident?" I begged him.

"Yes Grant," he said simply and softly and with that single "yes" I was relieved ever so slightly from my burden of guilt.

"Kai, is there any possible way I can ever make up for this mistake? Anything I can do to make repatriation to that little girl or her parents? Would the child have come here? Could any of them ever forgive me?"

"Possibly Grant, but I don't want to make any promises. What seems to be impossible in some places is often possible here but I have no control over what may or may not be. All I know is that you have suffered terribly and I pain for you," he said gently.

His empathy touched me to my core and I felt like weeping again.

"Thank you Kai," I managed to mumble before my emotions overcame me.

"Grant, tell me something. What symptoms did your body manifest during your life time? A body cannot endure such distress without trying to warn you of its turmoil."

"Well, come to think of it, I always had problems with a feeling of choking and insomnia was definitely an issue."

"Do you understand this is the way an organism screams of its abuse? Sleep is a way to resolve issues and air, freely inhaled, is the fullness of life. Without these two aspects of existence, life is severely compromised. No wonder it has taken you eighty-eight years to develop!" Kai exclaimed.

"What do you mean, eighty-eight years?" I gasped.

"Well, eighty-eight years in therapy of course. How long did you think you'd been here?"

To me, I felt as if I'd only been with Kai a few months, not eighty-eight years! It seemed as if time was spiralling away from me like water down a drain hole. On this occasion, I couldn't respond as before to the shock of the time continuum. My mind had had enough to deal with disclosing my confession. Numbed, devoid, robbed of all energy, I simply blanked out.

CHAPTER XIII

I dreamt a horrible, frightening dream, a nightmare which may have been triggered by my stressful disclosure. I dreamt that Laura and I had been poisoned and died in our sleep. In our Will, we had requested we be buried together in a double coffin in the eventuality that we both died at the same time.

After the funeral, as the gravediggers were shovelling dirt on top of the coffin, I regained consciousness. Realising my predicament, I started screaming at the top of my lungs, but to no avail. No-one could hear me. I listened as the thudding earth became fainter and fainter until finally I could hear it no longer.

The coffin was absolutely claustrophobic with the top of the coffin only inches from my face. It had taken a big effort just to twist my hands around to push on the lid. It was hopeless. The blackness was as impenetrable as the lid.

Time passed and I was surprised that there was still enough oxygen left to breathe. The air began to dissipate and I struggled for each breath. Somehow, there was just enough to ensure survival. My throat was parched from lack of water and my gasps for air. Uncomfortable as those feelings were, it was nothing compared to the mental anguish of the claustrophobia I was suffering. There was nothing to keep my mind occupied so there was nothing to distract me from my torment.

Hours turned into days, days into weeks and still I would not die. Meanwhile, Laura's decomposing corpse lay next to me, the stench unbelievable.

"Please end this, let me die!" I would beg silently.

There was no answer. This nightmare existence continued, endlessly struggling for breath, nothing to do, lying day by day next to a rotting body. Eventually, a tiny ray of light crept into the coffin, just enough for me to see my hands for a moment. The view chilled me to the bone and made me realise that the nightmare had only just started. There was no flesh on my hands. I finally understood I was just as dead as Laura and living the worst version of hell imaginable, trapped in a coffin for eternity.

When I awoke I was shaken but relieved to discover it was only a dream. It had all seemed way too real while I was experiencing it. I felt fragile and deeply disquieted.

"What could my strange dream possibly mean?" I wondered.

Kai arrived at exactly the right time to help me interpret my dark illusions. I relayed the dream from start to finish, still feeling haunted.

"Well done," Kai soothed me. "This dream is important for your continued progress."

"How could a dream like that help me?"

"Grant, to dream of your own funeral represents circumstances which you've been dealing with. It is the burying of emotions and aspects of yourself but your dream is telling you to pay attention to them. A dream of death is a way to help you deal with the loss of certain people.

"Being buried alive is a sign of mental anguish and the casket symbolises the finishing of a period of your life. To dream of being 'undead,' implies that you are being plagued with old thoughts which sabotage your happiness. All these are signs that you are ready to release yourself from old and nagging thought systems."

My spirits lifted immediately but I needed some time to digest the information.

"Is it all right to have a break? I need some time to gather my thoughts."

"Of course Grant. I will return when you are ready," Kai said as his Aura disappeared.

As soon as Kai had disappeared, Niara materialised in front of me. It was as if she had been waiting for an opportune moment.

"I see you Grant. How is your therapy progressing?"

"Hi Niara, it's great to see you again," I answered. "My therapy has been challenging, to say the least, but I've been learning a lot about myself and it made me realise, after all this time, I know almost nothing about you."

I felt guilty that I'd never inquired or shown any real consideration for Niara. I wondered if I'd been that way with other people who had been important in my life?

"What would you wish to know?" Niara asked, seemingly pleased with my interest.

"Well, everything, starting with your life on Earth."

"Very well, although there is probably not a lot to tell compared to your Earthly existence.

"I lived a relatively simple life with a large tribe in Central East Africa. When I was very young I was often involved in the gathering of food and water with the other women but sometimes we would join the men on the hunt for Kudu, Antelope, Dikdik or Buffalo.

"The gathering equipment we used was very basic but it was all we needed. A hide sling, a blanket and a cloak we called kaross to carry foodstuffs in and a digging stick. We would search for tubers, bush onions, fruit and berries as well as Ostrich eggs and insects such as grasshoppers, butterflies, termites and beetles. We would often use the ostrich egg shells to carry our water in.

"My clan would occasionally leave the tribe and wander the savannahs and jungles, searching for medicinal plants, precious stones, unusual delicacies and of course water. Are you aware Grant, that Africa is the hottest continent on Earth? Dry lands and deserts comprise sixty percent of the entire land surface and yet it still contains the most diversity of life found on the planet."

"I do vaguely recall Africa being the hottest and driest continent. Was water an issue where you were?"

"Water was often a problem, especially in spring when hot, dry periods would follow the cool, dry winter. Sometimes my people would need to resort to scraping a deep hole in damp sand and inserting a long hollow grass stem to suck the precious liquid up. Most plants were still dormant then and our supplies of nuts would be exhausted. Meat was very important to us at these times. We always gave thanks to the spirit of the animals that were killed.

"It was not all hard work though. Large amounts of time were spent in conversation, making up songs, painting and dancing, along with other rituals. The children could play to their hearts' content. Each child had a family name so there was not the range of names that are seen today. We were at peace with each other and the Earth. If there were any major problems, such as prolonged drought, we would ask Nyame for help."

"How would you do that?"

"An Okomfo would eat the rootbark of a tabernanthe iboga plant and enter the spirit world through a forced, self-induced trance. It was always a difficult journey and not to be taken lightly, but the visions the traveller would return with, though often terrifying and complex, would usually offer solutions. A trance journey was always undertaken for the good of the community," Niara concluded.

I had heard at some stage about different tribes around the world who would perform ceremonies calling for an individual to experience a deep, trance like state. I knew that Native Americans did what they called 'Vision Questing' after such ceremonies. They would then go to barely accessible places such as mountain tops and recreate the visions they had seen through rock art.

Humans have a hard-wired capacity to see geometric shapes known as form constants when in the lightest stages of trance. As the trance deepens, the subject attempts to make sense of the patterns and so they change into things that are governed by the individuals particular culture. Scientists believe these phenomena result in weird rock art traditions containing figures which are half human and half animal.

"Tell me more," I urged Niara, utterly fascinated. "Did you have any siblings?"

"Yes, two sisters, but I rarely saw them after they found partners in other clans. Their names were Ndidi, which means 'patience' and Ngozi, which means 'blessing' in our language. I do see them every now and again in the Afterlife which I thoroughly enjoy," she explained.

"Does Niara have a meaning?"

"Of high purpose," was her soft reply and I couldn't help but think what an apt name she held.

"How long ago did you live on Earth Niara?"

"A long, long time ago," she responded dreamily.

"How long is a long, long time?" I coaxed.

"Let me think. Yes, it would be around fifty thousand years ago."

"Fifty thousand years! I can't believe it. I had no idea. In my mind you sound so much younger. I wouldn't have believed you were a day over forty thousand years," I joked, partly to cover my shock.

My mind went into quick overdrive, trying to compute the information with my anthropological knowledge.

"Niara, that means you were alive when Neanderthals walked the planet!" I exclaimed, thrilled by this new development. "Did you ever meet any?"

"I am not sure Grant. I saw many strange people in my lifetime as we travelled far and wide. We would often avoid contact with other tribes in case they considered us trespassers. I do recall there were small groups who were shunned by the other tribes; perhaps they were your Neanderthals?"

"This is incredible. I can't imagine the changes you must have seen over such a long period. Did you often go back to Earth for a look?"

"Yes Grant, I have been back many times. When I was alive on Earth, none of us could ever have comprehended how dramatically the world would change," she said slightly wistfully.

"Did you ever marry?"

"Yes, I did eventually find a mate. I was much older than what was traditional for the time. I think I was considered a maverick by the elders. My partner, Afram, was a great hunter and a good man. We were only 'married' for a few years before he was killed by a rogue elephant while trying to save his friend."

"Oh, that was unfortunate. Did you ever have any children?"

"Yes, I was blessed with a daughter before Afram died. We named her Shani. It means Marvellous and it suited her personality perfectly."

All the talk of her life made me think of her death but I didn't know how to ask her this question without appearing utterly insensitive. Once more, Niara read what was on my mind for she continued her story.

"My daughter grew up quickly and found a mate in another group. My heart was sad to see her leave but I realised, for all tribes to remain strong, new blood had to be introduced. She quickly adapted and was soon pregnant with her first child. She was young and healthy, about thirteen years of age, so had an easy delivery with her daughter's birth.

"I adored my little grand-daughter. Her name was Aisha, which means 'She is Life'. I loved to watch her smile and would visit often, showing her the wonders of nature. Her laughter at the soft touch of a beetle or a butterfly delighted me. By the time she was making her first tentative steps, I was celebrating my fortieth year.

"One day, in the hard time of the year when life existed through the eating of meat, Shani's tribe came across a wounded antelope. Everyone was pleased because hunting was normally a long and arduous task. I was with the group at the time, baby-sitting little Aisha. I did not want the tribe to think I was interfering with their rituals, so I had moved well away with Aisha.

"The antelope was dispatched and as thanks were being given, a lion burst upon the scene. I could see he was thin and starving and guessed he was an old lion, too old to be a member of a pride and therefore an outcast. We all realised these are the most dangerous lions and the tribe scattered, all running as fast as they could, not realising I had been separated.

"With the heavy load of Aisha, my legs were not swift enough and the lion caught me from behind, knocking me to the ground. Aisha was flung from my arms and rolled into the grass where she stayed perfectly still, rigid with fear. My last thoughts were for my darling little grand-daughter. Mercifully, death came quickly and I was not left to suffer. The lion returned to the antelope and Shani was able to retrieve Aisha."

I didn't know what to say and silence hung between us like a shroud. Eventually, I managed to say a stumbling "Oh Niara," but Niara was serene.

"Grant, it was a very, very long time ago and you know that this is a place of peacefulness most of the time. I have drawn upon the energy of Nyame and I have calmness in my heart.

"Are you the oldest Being here?" I inquired.

"No Grant. The Ancient Ones are twice my age. They are my mentors. They have guided me through the Transitions and beyond, just as I will continue to guide you," she stated.

"Niara, what do you mean by 'and beyond' and how did all this start anyway? What is our purpose Niara?"

"All will be revealed soon but right now you need to finalise your therapy. Each step is a step forward and must be completed in order. Structure will give you your purpose," she stated enigmatically as she dissipated from my view.

"Wow, fifty thousand years!" I exclaimed, shaking my head in disbelief.

So far back in time, I wondered if Niara could even remember what her family looked like. Had their visages faded from her memory like a waning twilight, gently obscuring features which had once been so familiar? I started thinking of all the people I had known who had passed away and all the people that had been alive and were now almost certainly dead, even my grandchildren. Their faces floated before my mind's eye, a gallery of eyes, noses, lips and hair colour.

Some were people I'd cared for, others not so much. A few were close friends but there were many who had been just acquaintances. It surprised me that I still recalled so many of these people and in such detail. With each face that flitted before me, I was able to match a character trait.

There was Aunt Phoebe. Memories flooded back regarding her. I remember, oh so well, of playing cards with her and other family members. Always laughing, a twinkle in her eye, she had no regard for the sensibilities of youth. If we tarried too long mixing the cards we'd soon hear her colourful turn of phrase admonishing us "not to shuffle the tits off the queens."

And there was Grandpa. He was always playing jokes on us. I called him 'Rara' from the minute I could talk. Mum had an idea it was because of the sound of his car engine which I could apparently identify from a distance. He'd take us all fishing on the Campaspe River. On the trip there, he'd often yell out the window "Hello Harry." (Or Jack or Fred or whatever name he made up) We kids were always trouts. As soon as he threw the bait, we bit.

"Where's Harry? Who are you talking to Grandpa?" we'd ask, scared to miss a thing.

"Aw, he was just over there," he'd say, (or behind a bush or in a car that had passed etcetera etcetera) "you just missed him."

Even Dad paced before me, but this time the memories were of him taking us to the snow or to the beach. I could see him laughing at the cartoons on TV, or hear him as he whistled to the tunes on the radio which he kept by his side while he worked at odd jobs in the yard. I remembered him running up the highway chasing our cat, Ringo, after it had escaped from the car on our inaugural trip from Melbourne to Canberra. Dad returned triumphantly with the errant feline when we'd all thought he'd been lost for good.

That trip, where we'd almost lost Ringo, was an enjoyable memory. The house contents in Melbourne had been packed up, the moving truck sent on its way with our meagre possessions and what remained was rammed into and onto Dad's old Ford Prefect. Keira, Richard and I trilled with excitement, even though there wasn't enough room to put our legs down in the back seat area we shared with the cat.

We left later than intended, about mid-afternoon, so we only managed to reach the township of Echuca by day's end. It was the first time we three children had ever stayed in a hotel and we made the most of every second, exploring our room first, then the corridor, toilet and bathroom that we shared with several guests. Takeaway food was another unusual treat, so we were in seventh heaven. At the time, Keira was ten, Richard nine and I was seven.

The next day we left bright and early, stopping in Holbrook to repair the car's water pump and later in the day we had lunch in Albury. We took the cat for a walk on his collar and lead in the local park, much to the amusement of passers-by. Everyone was happy, enjoying the adventurous journey. Dad even took a leaf out of Grandpa's book by exclaiming,

"Look, a car with square tyres!"

As usual, we took the bait and were just about hanging out of our vehicle's windows, craning our necks for a look at the non-existent wonder.

We tootled on, mile after mile, until darkness fell. The stars were beautiful in the night sky. A toilet stop gave the cat his chance for the aforementioned sprint up the road and Dad's heroic dash to save him. Keira, Richard and I played 'I spy', sang songs and dozed where we could until eventually Dad spotted the lights of our new city, Canberra.

We pulled into the driveway at two o'clock in the morning. Mum ran a bath for the three of us and we were tucked into bed by four o'clock. The pitch blackness hid any signs of what our new environment would be like. At seven o'clock we hit the ground running, so anxious and excited were we to see our new home and backyard. The yard was enormous with Mt Ainslie looming above us to the rear of the house. Wide-eyed with wonder, we were overcome with delight at the prospects before us.

That mountain became our new backyard. We scaled it at every opportunity, as agile as mountain goats. We even managed to coerce Mum to climb with us a few times, a testament to her love for us. Our parents much preferred driving up in the car along the narrow winding road to enjoy the panoramic views from the top. Those early days were the start of a wonderful life which we would never have experienced if we had stayed in Melbourne. I had to be grateful to my father for that at least.

Kai's sudden appearance by my side startled me.

"How are you feeling now Grant?" were his first concerned words. "Have you gathered your thoughts?"

"Actually, yes I have and I'm feeling better for it."

"Well done. You have lanced the boil of guilt, remorse, stress and anxiety which was eating away at your psyche. Keep the wound open by recalling all and let the poison of your memories drain from you. Once the wound is cleaned of all impurities, then the healing will start. I think you need more time to reflect at the moment Grant. We will continue your therapies later," Kai stated considerately as once again he faded from view.

Already I was feeling more light-hearted. The burden I had carried for most of my life was slowly but surely being lifted from me. I began to look forward to becoming the person I could have been and should have been if not for the circumstances of my life. I felt as if I'd turned a corner and I was now on the road to recovery.

"Perhaps this is the start of my purpose?" I wondered. "Grant, it's quite amazing how your priorities have changed and what you thought your purpose would be," I muttered to myself.

I had to laugh at my burning ambition at age twenty to be financially independent by age forty. Yeah, I gave myself twenty years to get it all together and then I was going to be on the endless holiday in the sun.

When I reached forty and realised I was nowhere near fulfilling my goal, I hit a brick wall. Hard! I had to reassess everything and I found it a crippling and confronting task. I had to retreat to my man cave for a period but when I ventured forth, it was with renewed vigour. By the time I'd turned forty-five I was in the process of building a much bigger house for the family and my dreams had grown.

Laura and I became involved with a network marketing company and threw ourselves into meetings and presentations for the next six years. It was hard work and we were rorted in the end, but I have to admit the experience made me grow as a person. Never comfortable with public speaking in my younger days, I ended up becoming quite a proficient and self-confident presenter. Best of all, I met a lot of people that I never would have come in contact with and some became life-long friends.

It was good for Laura too. It helped keep her mind off the loss of her mother to a brain tumour a couple of years earlier and the fact that our nest was emptying. Casey started University in Mackay, a ten hour drive away. Chase left school after finishing year ten and started a bricklaying apprenticeship under me. He saved enough to buy a Toyota Supra Coupe that became his pride and joy. We didn't see a lot of him after that. He was too busy being out and about enjoying himself.

I was still thinking of my loved ones when Niara rejoined me. Realising it would be pointless to continue my previous line of questioning, I decided to change tack and find out about something else that had been playing on my mind since Kai's revelation.

"Niara, do you know what has been happening on Earth? Kai told me that I've been in therapy eighty-eight years now so that would make it around the year 2150, give or take a year. Is anyone still alive?"

Niara's aura brightened visibly.

"Grant, you will be very happy to know that life has improved dramatically on Earth. Valuable lessons have been learnt from the horrific sixties. So many lives were lost, even with our intervention. Half the human race died over a six year period before the smallpox virus was completely eradicated.

"Populations have stabilised since then, with few families having more than one child. Conflict between nations is virtually non-existent as countries have become borderless. With all nations working together, real poverty has almost ceased to exist. This lack of poverty has created virtually crimeless societies."

"Wow, things really have changed on Earth. I would never have believed they could have reduced poverty to that extent. What else has happened?"

"I'm sure this will interest you Grant. With the advent of artificially enhanced animals, humans are now able to communicate with a large variety of mammals, reptiles and birds. This completely changed most people's perspective on animals and their treatment. A huge humanitarian movement for animals was established and on the 29th of November 2128, legislation was passed making it illegal to kill animals for human consumption, sport or cosmetic experimentation."

"That seems to be quite an over-reaction, people not being allowed to eat meat."

"Perhaps Grant. Although once it was proven that animals had similar emotions to humans it became difficult to argue a case for breeding animals to be slaughtered. Also, all the meat is grown synthetically nowadays, so most of the old farming practices have become obsolete."

"What about hunting?"

"Hunting is done by animatronics. They are absolutely lifelike robotic animals which can be hunted in various game reserves. The benefits of using animatrons apart from not harming animals are the range is unlimited and the animals can be programmed to suit an individual's level of expertise. A person can hunt anything from a quail to a tyrannosaurus rex. They also have another version of hunting which is called halo hunting. It is a similar concept to hunting animatrons except the animals are holograms and the hunter uses a laser gun. That can even be done inside buildings."

"Gee whiz, that sounds like a lot of fun. I was never interested in hunting when I was alive but that seems like something even I would have loved to have tried. So what have they done about fishing Niara?"

"They do have similar animatronic fishing reserves where a person can fish the entire range from modern to prehistoric. They also compromised about natural fishing. Anglers may use hookless lures which chemically weld to the fish's mouth. The lures release an anaesthetic which ensures the fish doesn't feel any pain in its mouth and must be released upon capture. Studies have shown the fish does get distressed but quickly recovers so at the moment this style of fishing has been deemed acceptable."

"But they can't eat fish?"

"Fish meat along with every other meat is grown synthetically. There is no need to kill the animal."

"That's really interesting. What other technological advances have been made?"

"In science, nanotechnology has reached new heights. Molecular robotics have been programmed to create everything from toys, to cars, to skyscrapers. In the field of medicine, nanobots, atom sized robots, have been developed which are being used to repair and restructure cells. Any disabilities are repairable. Limbs are being regrown, eyesight and hearing restored and spinal cords reconnected, along with countless other formerly degenerative diseases. In fact, almost all diseases have been controlled and the average lifespan is now two hundred and thirty-five years. People who are one hundred look and feel as if they are thirty."

If I'd had a mouth, it would have been hanging open as Niara continued.

"People have become extremely conscious of the environment. Nothing is done without considering the impact on nature. After having lost eighty percent of the Amazon rainforest by the 2060s, the area was heritage listed and now, less than ninety years later, with the help of nanotechnology, the Amazon rainforest has been returned to its former glory. All pollution has been transformed into environmentally friendly products, thanks to advancements in science.

"Motor vehicles have changed quite dramatically and are exhaust free. By using a combination of anti-gravity and electricity, a generator using a frictionless electro-magnetic prime mover spins so rapidly that it makes the object weightless. With this movement it also produces enough electricity to power any number of electric motors. The motors can propel these weightless vehicles to incredible velocities and produce no pollution. The generators are self-sustained so no outside power supply is ever required."

"They finally got flying cars," I mused.

"And in fashion, invisibility suits are all the rage at the moment. Light weight fabric clothes can bend light in three dimensions making the wearer appear to be completely invisible. There are still a few glitches with them apparently; they lose their effect in water or inclement weather.

"Oh, and the moon has now been populated. It has cities which are completely enclosed under massive glass domes. It is a very popular destination for honeymooners where they can watch the Earth from the comfort of their hotel rooms. I think that would be a lovely experience. Do you agree Grant?"

"Yes I do. That would be a great way to start a marriage."

"And now finally, I get to tell you the best news of all. For the first time in recorded history, there are no wars on the planet. For the time being, humans are actually at peace," Niara concluded.

I couldn't believe it. Humanity had been on the brink of extinction, with their backs against the wall, when we had gone back to intervene. Now, less than one hundred years later, not only had they recovered but they had managed to achieve the impossible. Borderless countries, no wars, poverty or crime should have been unachievable pipe-dreams, but somehow this generation of people had done just that and created miracles in the process. Who would have believed it?

"That is the most wonderful news I've ever heard. Thank you so much Niara for making me aware of these stupendous events. Now I can truly go back to therapy with a lighter heart!"

CHAPTER XIV

*E*ach therapy session spent with Kai was a blessing. He had a way about him that I could relate to and I could feel myself opening up in a way I would have never thought possible. Each meeting was a period of discovery and I began to have feelings of real self-worth. I decided it was about time I should thank him for all his hard work, so with deep gratitude I began.

"Kai, I just want to let you know how much I appreciate you and what you're doing for me..."

Before I could go any further he'd hushed me but I knew he was pleased.

"In the words of a man of the Earth, 'We may define therapy as a search for value'," he kindly stated. "Grant, did you ever hear of a psychologist by the name of Abraham Maslow? He was the man who first used those words."

I thought about it for a minute then answered him with,

"Wasn't he the guy that came up with a visual model of what he called a 'Hierarchy of Needs'?"

"Yes Grant, he's the one. What do you know of his model?"

"Well, if I've got it right, his idea was that humans need to have certain needs met before they can fully realise their potential. If those needs aren't met then the person can't move forward. They're stuck on that level."

"That's correct Grant. Do you remember what the levels were?"

"I remember a few, but I may require help remembering all of them. As far as I recall, the bottom level was the basic physiological needs of a human which are food, water and sex. The next level had to do with safety. A person needs security, order and stability which are important for the physical survival of each individual. Once a person has basic nutrition, shelter and safety, the person attempts to accomplish more by sharing themselves with others. That level is the third level, the level of love and belonging. I know there's more but I can't remember what comes after that," I concluded.

"Excellent!" Kai praised. "The fourth level is the esteem level, when a person is comfortable with what they've accomplished and not unduly influenced by others. The final level is when a person has reached a state of harmony and understanding which Maslow named 'Need for Self- Actualization'.

"These people have extraordinary 'peak' experiences. They are more aware of justice, truth and goodness. According to Maslow, these humans have Being values during their peak experiences. He listed these values as wholeness, perfection, completion, aliveness, richness, simplicity, beauty, goodness, uniqueness, effortlessness, playfulness, truth and self-sufficiency. However, these experiences were often climactic, emotional and short-lived.

"They were necessary for the journey toward the 'plateau' experience, a far more voluntary process than the involuntary process of 'peaks'. The person could see in a unitive way almost at will. This sense then became a witnessing, an appreciating, a blissfulness which had an air of casualness and lounging about. It was sereneness and calmness, a time of pure enjoyment, of marvelling, wondering and philosophising.

"The 'plateau' can only be achieved, learnt and earned by work, study, discipline and commitment. His ideas were discredited by other psychologists until many years after he had died. Eventually, his concept was re-visited and as you are aware, the human race was able to correct its wrong thinking."

"Maslow based his ideas on the writings of Albert Einstein, the ideology of Lao Tzu, the father of Taoism and people whom he met who had achieved the level of self-actualization. I'm telling you this Grant because I think you will understand his thought processes and because he absolutely loathed his mother. You, on the other hand, feared and disliked your father intensely. If Maslow could come to the understandings that he did, given his feelings toward his mother, then I believe you will find what he had to say relevant to yourself."

"Kai, do you know anything about Maslow's background and why he hated his mother?"

"Yes, as a matter of fact I do."

"He was the eldest of seven children born to Jewish Russians who immigrated to America. As for his mother, he didn't have a kind word to say about her and I quote, 'What I had reacted to and totally hated and rejected was not only her physical appearance, but also her values and world view, her stinginess, total selfishness, her lack of love for anyone in the world; even her own children and husband, her narcissism, Negro prejudice, her exploitation of everyone, her assumption that anyone was wrong who disagreed with her, her lack of friends, sloppiness and dirtiness'. I guess that just about sums it all up," Kai finished.

"Phew! And I thought I had it in for Dad," I exclaimed. "Do you think it was because of his mother he became a psychologist?"

"Perhaps Grant. Abraham obviously had the fortitude to investigate human relationships and maybe it was his own personal relationship which provided the catalyst. His insight into the makings of the human psyche showed a diligence and understanding rare in most mortals. Would you like to know what Maslow's eight behaviours leading to self-actualization were Grant?"

"Of course I would. If there is anything that will help me I would love to know."

"Very well... The first was concentration. Self- actualisation means experiencing fully and completely, with one hundred percent concentration and total absorption. Usually we are relatively unaware of what is going on within or around us. Most eyewitnesses recount different versions of the same occurrence. However, we all have moments of heightened awareness and intense involvement; moments that Maslow would call self-actualising.

"The second behaviour was growth choices. Consider life as a series of choices. Each choice you make can be made on the basis of safety or growth. Making safe choices may stultify your opportunities to grow as a person although it will lessen the risk of failure. Self-actualisation is to choose growth and to open yourself to new and challenging experiences, even though you risk the unknown and possible failure.

"The third was self-awareness. This is where we start trusting ourselves and become more aware of our inner nature and act in accordance with it. This means we decide for ourselves whether we like certain films, books or ideas, regardless of whether our peers approve or have differing opinions.

"The fourth behaviour was honesty and taking total responsibility for ourselves and our actions. Rather than make calculated responses that we think may please the recipient to make ourselves look good, we can look within for the answers. Each time we do so, we get in touch with our inner selves.

"Number five was judgement. The first four steps help us develop the capacity for 'better life choices'. We decide to trust our own judgment and follow our own instincts. When this is achieved, one will find that better choices are made throughout our lives in areas such as marriage, career, music, books and philosophies.

"The sixth behaviour was self-development. This is a continual process of developing one's potentialities. It means harnessing one's abilities and intelligence to achieve the things you most desire. Great talent or intelligence is not the same as self-actualisation; many gifted people fail to use their abilities fully while others, with perhaps only average talents, accomplish a great deal.

"The seventh you will recall was peak experiences, which are transient moments of self-actualisation. During these peak moments we are more whole and fully aware of ourselves, enabling us to think, act and feel more clearly and accurately. We experience more love, compassion and empathy during these moments and have less inner conflict and anxiety.

"Finally, the eighth behaviour was lack of ego defences. This is the ability to recognise when our egos have put up barriers and then are able to drop them when we feel appropriate. Our ego defences often distort our own images and the way we perceive the external world. Self-analysis is the key and a further step in self-actualisation of ego defences. When you think about it, much of this relates to you Grant," Kai stated earnestly.

"Yes, I can see now why Niara said I was a long way from attaining inner peace," I mumbled. "Was Maslow a religious man Kai?"

"Not in an orthodox way Grant, but he had a connection with Nyame without really knowing it. Quite remarkably, for a man of his time, he was able to understand what only earlier mankind had felt. He stated, 'The sacred is in the ordinary. It is to be found in one's daily life, one's neighbours, friends and family, in one's backyard. To be looking for miracles is to me a sure sign that everything is miraculous'. Yes, he was able to understand that Nyame is part of everything and that man has a higher and transcendent nature and this is part of his essence," Kai finished.

"I'm really going to have to spend some time letting this sink in," I apologised to Kai, gob-smacked by all the information he had attached to his thinking.

"That's fine Grant. We have plenty of time, an eternity of it. You don't have to rush. Oh, and by the way, thank you for your words of gratitude. They meant a lot and show how far you've come," he complimented me.

Strangely, at that moment, I recalled one other thing I'd read about Maslow.

"Kai, do you think Maslow really understood what he was saying when he warned people against rejection of the guide, the teacher, the sage, the therapist, the counsellor, the helper along the path to self-actualization and the realm of Being?"

I shuddered at the thought that I would have been just the sort of person to have believed Maslow's ideas were bizarre.

"I believe he only understood in a sub-conscious way. It is an innate urge to belong to Nyame. Every man, woman and child can find that feeling at the core of themselves. Sadly, there are few who tap the bounty and bring it forth."

It was with a sense of awe I reflected on Abraham Maslow's words, astounded he could so accurately describe what Niara and Kai were, without having experienced death. How had he known that we would need a guide, a teacher, a helper along the path to self-actualisation and the realm of Being?

"Was it a lucky guess? Did he mean something else, or did he just know?" I pondered. "I hope I meet the guy one day so I can ask him."

Time meandered and Kai had me explore every thought, action and word I'd ever uttered, shining new meaning on what I'd believed I knew and understood.

"Feel for your father, not against him," he counselled me. "Get inside the mind of the man and find the frightened child, the one brought up without a Dad when all his peers wallowed in their father's love. Understand the difficulty of expressing a father's love to a child without knowing what that love was," Kai urged. "Delve deep into the pool of forgiveness, swim in it, bathe in it, feel it soothe the anger and hurt from your inner self. After that, forgive yourself."

"I didn't do anything to hurt my father," I responded, half as a statement and half as a question, surprised he could suggest such a thing.

"Oh, but you did Grant. You never gave the love that is a father's due nor thanks for the sacrifices he did make to sustain you. With the selfishness of a child, you saw what was apparent to you but you did not grow. Your negative attitudes became habitual. Do you realise that you and your siblings had the power to save your father with love?"

Those words hit me like a sledge hammer. An image shot into my head when my first child Casey was born. I hadn't even let my father know of his grandchild's birth. A month later, I received a package containing a beautiful pink baby's outfit with a card congratulating me. I never responded. Less than three years later, he hung himself.

How could I have been so cruel and unforgiving? Because of his faults, I had allowed myself to react in the same thoughtless manner. I felt that my inaction had a direct impact on his demise and it was as if I had tied the noose around his neck.

For the first time in my life I examined my father. Every moment I could think of seeped into my mind, snaking into my consciousness in a thousand different ways. Buried in my innermost parts I began to 'feel' for my father, finding a few admirable qualities that I'd quashed in my ambition to find nothing favourable about him. With this realisation came release. I found myself ebbing away from my Dad, freed from my bitter emotions and joyful calm settled on my heart.

"Grant, you are doing so well, I've decided there is someone I want you to meet," Kai told me not too long after my revelations regarding my father.

Spontaneously, I found myself before a Being I hadn't met before.

"Grant, I'd like you to meet Kathleen. Kathleen, this is Grant. Grant is the one who killed your daughter," Kai explained, seemingly unaware of the bombshell he'd just dropped.

I felt as if I'd been hit with a lightning bolt. Electrified with shame and remorse, I stood rooted to my position, awaiting the tirade of abuse which must surely come my way. Kathleen's aura remained steady and bright. The only indication she gave of having heard this expose was a gentle "Oh," as soft as an exhaled breath, holding no rancour or sorrow.

I wanted Kathleen's forgiveness so badly I could taste it, but I couldn't utter a word of repentance. Struck dumb with my horror of the situation, all I could do was mutely await whatever Kathleen would say or do next.

My mind churned, thinking, "How could Kai do this to me without warning?"

It took some seconds to realise that Kathleen's thoughts were trickling into my consciousness like a crystal clear stream.

"Grant, I have wanted to meet you for a very long time but Kai did not think you were ready. I am pleased to see he must now believe the time is right for us to speak. From what Kai has told me, I understand that your distress has been great regarding the death of Tara. Is there anything you would like to say to me?"

Her gentle question at last loosened the restrictive bonds which had been gagging me.

"Oh Kathleen, I'm so very, very sorry for what I must have put you through. I know how devastated I would have been if it was one of my children. You have suffered so much because I was a selfish coward. I was too concerned with my own wellbeing to contemplate the impact of my actions on you. I know you could never forgive me, nor do I deserve forgiveness, but I want you to know from the centre of my being, how truly regretful I am. If there was any way to undo that day and my actions thereafter, I would do it in an instant."

"Ah Grant, I know that and you are wrong. I do forgive you. Yes, those many years of not knowing where Tara was, created an ache in my heart until my dying day, but Tara has told me she believes what happened to her was for the best," was her astounding reply.

"You mean you've been reunited with your daughter here?" I asked, scarcely daring to hope this was the case.

"Yes Grant, it is true," answered Kathleen, as the last vestige of poisonous emotions which had gripped me during my life drained away. "Tara was a troubled child, full of anxiety, anger and rebellion. She truly believes that had she lived her life to the full, she would have been responsible for many misdeeds, pain and suffering. Tara has expressed gratitude that her life was cut short by an unforeseen accident which prevented her from causing harm to others. She has been blissfully happy here and is progressing well in her transitions," Kathleen ended.

What a wonder this was to me. I couldn't believe the event which had crippled me as a person could possibly end this way. Kathleen's forgiveness, her renewed relationship with her daughter and the knowledge of Tara's acceptance of what had happened, washed through me like a cleansing summer storm. I felt utterly humbled with gratitude at their loving reactions to my disastrous choices made so many years ago.

I realised that during all my therapy sessions with Kai, I had slowly but surely been emptied of all the corrupt thoughts of my former life and with this final act of exoneration, I was now filling with all the values of a Being. Like a tidal wave surging forward, filling every vacant space, I felt truth, love, honesty, joy and contentment and finally, a deep fulfilling joining to Nyame.

"Thank you! Thank you! Thank you!" was all the words I could find to say.

CHAPTER XV

Niara! How wonderful to see you. It's been so long since we've been together. How are you?"

My words tumbled and tripped out of my mouth in my excitement at seeing Niara again.

"I am well Grant and glad to see you also. It has been over seventy years since we last met. Your therapy is now complete and you appear in very good spirits."

"Ha! Ha! 'Spirits'? I thought I'd established I was the comedian out of the two of us? But yes Niara, I feel great. I'm ready to take on whatever purpose I've been prepared for. Am I now able to find out what my objective is and how everything started? When you told me the oldest Beings were born one hundred thousand years ago it seemed like such an odd period. Why back then? Is that when people first started to become Beings? What is Nyame's involvement and where is it all going? How does it work?" I asked her, bombarding her with the questions I'd been storing for so long.

Niara laughed.

"Grant, in one way you have not changed a bit in all this time. You are still overflowing with questions. I believe I can finally answer almost all your queries now so let me take you on a journey.

"One hundred thousand years ago, Nyame decided that humans were the perfect candidates for an experiment. We had evolved to a reasonable degree of intelligence and had shapes which could express that intelligence very easily."

"Would it matter what shape we were?"

"Well yes Grant. If you put a human brain into the body of a dolphin, for all intents and purposes, you still have a dolphin. In that animal shape, living in a watery environment, it would be very difficult to exhibit the capacity to acquire and utilise knowledge."

"I see what you mean. Niara, earlier you mentioned we evolved? Did you mean from hominids?"

"Yes of course, Grant. However, this is what you always believed, was it not?"

"Yes I did, but when I discovered an Afterlife existed I didn't know what to believe. I thought I might be wrong about everything. I must admit it's comforting to know that my love of science wasn't completely wasted."

It's funny; when I was alive I would have been doing cartwheels at the revelation that there could be no more arguments on whether evolution was real or not. Now, it seems quite irrelevant compared to the bigger picture.

"It just goes to show, there was a possibility science and religion could have worked together way back then after all," I reflected.

Niara continued, "Humans also had one other very necessary attribute. They have relatively short life spans."

"Why was it necessary for us to have short life spans?"

Niara responded in her calm, unflustered way.

"Nyame needs a maximum of five years to ensure the essence, or what people on Earth would call a soul, hasn't been badly corrupted. After five years of a human hosting Nyame's essence, it is irrelevant how long the body survives, or in other words, how long a person lives for."

"I'm sorry Niara; I'm not quite grasping this."

"That is all right Grant. Let me explain how people obtain their essence and then it may be clearer for you. One hundred thousand years ago, Nyame took some of its energy and placed it directly into all the newborn humans on Earth. By doing so, Nyame made humans the first creatures in the Universe to become immortal. However, when Nyame passes its energy into a human, the energy becomes slightly corrupted in the transfer. For virtually one hundred percent of mankind, that corruption is able to be neutralised. That is why you must go through the transition phases," she said.

"You said 'virtually'? Does that mean for a very few, the corruption can't be neutralised?"

"That is correct. A minuscule amount fails. Nothing in the universe is absolutely perfect," Niara concluded.

"Do those who fail go to Hell?"

"No Grant, there is no Hell. The concept of Hell was created by Church leaders in an effort to control people. Do you honestly believe Nyame would go to the trouble of transferring its energy into humans, making them immortal, only to have them suffer for an eternity in a place of torture for something as ridiculous as perhaps going to the 'wrong' church? No, you are far more valuable than that," Niara finished emphatically.

"That's a relief. So, how bad do you have to be to belong to this small percentage?"

"Nyame can tell after a child has turned five years of age whether the essence of that child has been completely corrupted or not. With human life forms, corruption is easily expressed and identified. There is a huge difference between someone who has been conditioned to behave badly and those whose essence has been completely corrupted.

"An absolutely depraved essence becomes the anti-matter of Nyame. The love, peace and compassion Nyame imbibes are replaced with hate, disharmony and a complete lack of empathy. One look into the eyes of a human with a consummately corrupted essence and you will see and feel pure evil," Niara finished warningly.

Her vivid description made me shudder and I was thankful I had never come across such an individual during my life time. I'd certainly heard about people who acted in ways that were abhorrent, sadistic and perverse and had often wondered how they could possibly be that way. Now I had the answer, terrible as it was.

"What happens to these people once Nyame has identified them?"

Niara's shocking answer was, "Sadly, they are annihilated."

"But if Nyame is love, peace and compassion, how could it do that?" I asked incredulously.

"Nyame does not annihilate," Niara replied firmly. "Grant, do you recall when I explained that a defiled essence is virtual anti-matter?"

At my affirmation she continued.

"When the human dies and their corrupt essence attempts to begin the transitions and rejoin with Nyame in the spirit world, on entering, its particles are the exact opposite of the particles it comes in contact with. At a touch, they are instantly destroyed. It is simply a question of chemistry," she stated matter-of-factly.

I was beginning to feel I was getting a grip on what Niara was trying to reveal. The pieces of the jigsaw were gradually coming together. I decided to try a different query in my quest for understanding.

"With Nyame placing bits of its energy into every human being, does it ever run the risk of becoming depleted of energy or matter?"

"That is a good question Grant. You need not worry though. The amount of energy rendered to each individual is miniscule. Besides that, Nyame is expanding with the Universe, nearly at the speed of light. There is unquestionably no danger that Nyame's power or energy will decrease."

"Niara, you said Nyame needs five years to test the essence of a person. What happens to the children who don't live to five years of age?"

Her simple answer surprised me.

"They are re-birthed."

"Re-birthed? Whatever do you mean by that?"

"If a child does not survive to five years of age, their essence is placed into new babies until they acquire the requisite number of years," was her profound revelation.

The fact that death was so indiscriminate had aligned with my former beliefs that no Supreme Being was involved with life on Earth. Death never seemed to favour whether you were good or bad, religious or not, or how hard you prayed. Death appeared to be completely random. More light had been shone on the confusing events of life which had surrounded me.

"Can Nyame intervene in anything on Earth?"

"Yes Grant. It has the power to do so but it would be extremely rare for Nyame to ever intervene. There is generally no need to. The intervention to save people from the smallpox epidemic was the first time we have ever been physically involved in people's daily lives. However, that was an extreme circumstance. Normally, we Guides can fix anything which people suffer on Earth through therapy. Some people may just need an extraordinary amount of time," she laughed and I sensed she was teasing me.

With admirable restraint I ignored the gentle jibe and continued with my search for answers.

"When do babies acquire their essence?"

"Just prior to delivery is the optimum time."

"Are there any babies who ever miss out?"

Niara could hardly contain her laughter to answer me.

"No Grant. Nyame is everywhere and in all things. Nothing is missed. Ever!"

"So there are no secrets, nothing that Nyame ever misses?" I asked sceptically.

"I am afraid not Grant. Everything you have ever experienced, every word you have ever muttered, every thought you have ever had, every smell you have ever smelt and every feeling you have ever felt is recorded in your subconscious which Nyame can access if required. Remember also, Nyame is part of everything, even the air you breathed.

"Mmm, knowing someone was there watching your every move could dull the mood for a lot of people in bed at night," I thought to myself wryly. "You said you and the other Guides go back to Earth sometimes. What do you do there?"

"Generally, we just observe. The human race's lifestyle changes so rapidly that in order for us to be able to help people to the best of our abilities, it is beneficial for us to see some of the trials and tribulations from each era that people are subjected to."

"Did you ever observe me? Were you my Guide even before I died? Was my death pre-ordained?" I interrogated her.

"I can only answer one question at a time Grant," Niara stated. "I may have observed you but I was not your Guide then and no-one's death is planned. You need to understand, in the big scheme of eternal life, what happens on Earth does not really have much relevance. A person gets some life experience which may be helpful in some cases or may be detrimental in others. For instance, a young person tends to make it through the transitions and complete their therapy faster than an elderly person. The young person is not as rigid in their thought processes and tends to have less mental baggage.

"Your death was random just like everyone else's. Nyame, being entwined with space time, allows the provision of being able to move back and forth through time. Nyame can shift to the future and observe your death before you actually experience it. However, it is one thing to observe, quite another to intervene. Intervention could be extremely dangerous."

"How could it possibly be dangerous?"

"You will have to have your wits about you to understand this," Niara cautioned. "The near future is still the past of the distant future and the distant future is still the past of a more distant future. If you change the past you may completely change the future and that may prove to be a disaster. You may find people in the future disappearing right before your eyes," she exclaimed.

"You're right Niara, that's way too confusing for me to comprehend right now. Talking about the past, were any of the religions right or wrong in their teachings of what was happening and what we were to expect? And where does science fit in to the scheme of things?"

"Why would you wish to know something like that?" Niara asked, seemingly surprised at my need to acquire this counsel.

"I know this might sound crazy to you and I realise it's probably irrelevant," I started, "but I want to know everything and if I'm to be a Guide one day, that information might prove to be useful."

Her measured answer caught me unawares.

"In a sense Grant, all of religion and science held some truths but they both suffered from rigid conformity. The advantage ancient races and civilisations had over people of your era, was that we knew unquestionably there was something greater than us and we could feel that knowledge and belief deep inside us. We could sense our soul. We did not know how it got there but we knew it was there. Did you not find it strange that every tribe and every civilisation in the entire world believed in something bigger than themselves?

"Yes, it did make me wonder occasionally."

"In my time," Niara continued, "we told stories of what the Afterlife might be. We had burial ceremonies, sacred places and paintings. Later, other civilisations were able to write down their ideas. No-one could know how everything was started or how Nyame and the transitions worked, but they knew something was there. They were able to sense the connection with Nyame.

"They explained their understanding in the best way they could, to suit their era and culture. Each tribe or nation had an intrinsic need to do this. The need to explain the inexplicable, to explain something they could feel with every fibre of their bodies."

"So that's why there are so many different religions and sects," I exclaimed. "Each group are feeling exactly the same thing but just describing it differently."

"That is correct Grant," Niara confirmed.

"How sad is that?" I muttered thoughtfully. "All that hatred and bloodshed, covering hundreds and thousands of years between differing religious groups, and it turns out they all really believe in the same thing."

"Yes Grant. It is quite sad. Fortunately, no-one lives long on Earth and when they get here, they learn the error of their ways, just as you did. Science faces similar problems with their rigid doctrines.

"Because Nyame came into existence at the same time as the beginning of the universe and because Nyame rarely involves itself in the natural world, its existence cannot be measured. In science, if it cannot be measured or tested, it does not exist. Science will continue to make inroads into the natural world but it has a long way to go in the supernatural world."

"I see what you mean and that's very interesting. What of the people involved with paranormal events like clairvoyance, channelling, astrology or astral projection? Are they actually managing to connect here?"

"Grant, what do you know of these things? Perhaps if you explain them to me you will discover the answer yourself."

"Okay. For a start, I know astral travel is often associated with near death experiences and people have the feeling of being outside of their bodies looking down. Some feel they are making an ascent to a higher realm, much as I did when I died. I read once about a singer by the name of Pam Reynolds whose out of body experience was well documented.

"Apparently she had a brain aneurysm which needed surgical repair and the only way the doctor could do the operation was to do a standstill. That is, her body temperature was lowered to sixty degrees Fahrenheit, her breathing and heartbeat were stopped and the blood was drained from her head. Her eyes were closed with tape and she had small ear plugs with speakers inserted into her ears and then covered with mounds of tape and gauze. The ear plugs emitted audible clicks which were used to check the function of the brain to ensure it was non-responsive before the operation proceeded. By all accounts she was clinically dead.

"The amazing part of this story was that she was able to describe the operation and what the doctors and nurses were saying. Pam said she heard a sound like a natural 'D' which seemed to pull her from her body and enabled her to float around the theatre. She reported she felt more aware than normal and that her focus and vision were clearer than ever before. At some point during the operation, she noticed a presence and she was pulled towards a light where she was able to discern former deceased relatives and people unknown to her, who fed her, not with food but with something sparkly which nurtured her and made her feel strong.

"The longer she stayed within this light, the more she enjoyed herself, but she was told she needed to return to her body. When she saw her body, it looked dead and she was afraid of it. Pam refused again and again to return, but at the point the doctors used defibrillation to restart her heart, one of her relatives pushed her back into her body. The sensation, Pam said, was like jumping into icy water.

"Then there are the people who claim to see auras. They say that each human has an astral body connected to it and this is what they can see. The colours of the aura indicate a precise emotional and physical state and I could certainly see the difference in our auras when I first met you Niara. Mine was so diluted with the aggravations to my essence that I hardly glowed at all."

How ignorant I'd been back then.

"Continue Grant," Niara encouraged.

"Well, I read a book once, written by Charles Fort, which intrigued me. His book on the paranormal used extracts that were originally reported in scientific journals such as 'Scientific American', 'Nature' and 'Science' and also newspapers like the 'The Times'. These reported events covering everything from teleportation, poltergeist events, falls of frogs, fish and other organic materials, crop circles, unaccountable noises and explosions, spontaneous fires, ball lightning, UFOs, levitation, mysterious appearances and disappearances and alien abductions. I always felt there must be a logical explanation for all these events; however some of them were very hard to explain.

"I figured there must be some substance to paranormal activity when I learnt of the Stargate Project which was established by the U.S Federal Government to investigate claims of psychic phenomena from the1970s through to 1995. This was around the time that Uri Geller became famous for his ability to apparently bend objects and stop and start watches using the power of his mind.

"The Central Intelligence Agency decided to check the viability of using 'remote viewing' psychics, those that purported the ability to see events and sites from a great distance, for information gathering operations. I thought the review at the termination of the project was interesting where it stated, 'Even though a statistically significant effect has been observed in the laboratory, it remains unclear whether the existence of a paranormal phenomenon has been demonstrated'.

"I'd discussed this project with Noel and Dave on the golf course one time and Noel came up with a quote he'd read, 'Approaching the paranormal from a research perspective is often difficult because of the lack of acceptable physical evidence from most of the purported phenomena. By definition, the paranormal does not conform to conventional expectations of nature. Therefore, a phenomenon cannot be confirmed as paranormal using the scientific method because, if it could be, it would no longer fit the definition'.

"We'd had a bit of a laugh with that one. It was almost a case of 'damned if you do or damned if you don't'. Now that I think of it, you were saying the exact same thing earlier."

"That is correct. Please go on Grant."

"NASA also commissioned studies into psychokinesis experiments, which investigated how human consciousness influences the behaviour of external physical systems. These studies were dropped when procedural problems and researcher conflicts became apparent that possibly skewed the results of the tests. This became a blot on the methodology and biasness of some of the participating scientific researchers. Sadly Niara, top dollar funding has been the cause of many scientists jigging results to keep the money pouring in, but I'm sure you are well aware of human frailties in the pursuit of fame and fortune."

"Yes Grant, that is all too true. Is there anything else you can tell me?"

"When I was younger, I watched a movie called the Exorcist which was quite horrific for those days. It made enough of an impression on me, that when I discovered it had been based on a true story, I did some research which I found quite fascinating. The information I came up with showed that an only child, a boy named Robbie, who was born to a German Lutheran couple living in Maryland in the United States in the 1940s, became demon possessed after the death of his aunt, who had introduced him to a Ouija board and her ideas as a spiritualist.

"Strange events began happening such as streaks, arrows and the word 'hell' appearing on the child's skin. Furniture and objects moved of their own accord and unusual sounds such as squeaky shoes and marching feet could be heard. Forty-eight witnesses came forward to confirm these happenings.

"Over the course of two months, the exorcism ritual was performed thirty times by various clergymen attempting to rid the boy of whatever it was that induced him to speak in a demoniacal voice, defecate on the walls and cause objects to smash and fly around. Eventually, three Jesuit priests performed the final exorcism in a psychiatric ward at a hospital. During the rite, one of the priests had his nose broken by Robbie. At the completion, a noise like a shotgun or thunderclap was heard throughout the hospital and the child declared, 'It's over. It's over.'

"Interestingly, the family were never troubled again by any of the phenomena and Robbie grew up to become a successful, happily married man, a father and grandfather. Close friends of the child claimed he was simply a spoiled, disturbed bully who threw deliberate tantrums to get attention and to get out of school. Who knows?

"I remember Keira, Richard and I used to hold a few séances. We gave them up when a glass we were using to spell out messages flew from our fingers and smashed into a thousand pieces. There was also a time after a séance had finished and Richard and I were getting ready for bed. The dog entered the room and went berserk, barking incessantly while staring up at a corner of the ceiling. I've never seen any dog act like that. He seemed to be terrified, yet there was nothing there. I just don't understand Niara. There are too many weird things that people get involved in," I finished, defeated in my confusion.

Niara's liquid laughter trickled through my mind.

"Oh Grant. Do not be downhearted. The answers are simple. Do you remember I once said that 'you have the power to move mountains' if you wish?"

"Yes, of course I remember."

"Well, the essence of Nyame within the individual enables many inexplicable things to be easily explained. Were you not told by scientists that humans only use one tenth of their brain capacity? The so-called unusual events you have described are only a diminutive accessing of part of the power available to each and every human. It is just that some individuals have stumbled on a way to use a little more of their essence and that connection to their brain than others have," she explained.

"So, are you telling me all supernatural events are the product of our own minds? That we are responsible for even the bad effects, such as with the child Robbie?" I asked incredulously.

"Yes Grant. You must realise that a child's brain is immature and they do not have the same control as an adult. It is a very frightening experience for a child to unlock some of the forces within their essence."

I couldn't help but agree with that statement. Niara had left me with plenty to contemplate. What a wonderful experience this has been so far. Thank heavens I was proven wrong about my atheist beliefs. This is SO much better than rotting in the ground.

CHAPTER XVI

Niara told me that sometime soon I would be facing a new transition. What it was I didn't know but I was sure there would be lessons in it for me. Here, there always seems to be a new lesson which has to be learnt from every occasion. Funny how I'd thought most of my lessons were behind me by the time I'd reached sixty years of age. Now, all I could see on reflection was that I had been but a babe in the scheme of things, a helpless infant with the understanding of a gnat.

The forces of life had been swirling around me, evident in a million ways, but I had been blinded to what had been placed directly in front of me. It was like when I'd look for the butter in the fridge and couldn't see it even though it would be prominently displayed. Laura would often laugh and comment with, "That butter could bite your hand off if you got any closer."

I wondered if that was how some of the different religious organisations had gotten off track. The truth was there in front of them but they were often sightless.

By the time I'd reached my fifties, I'd virtually stopped discussing religion all together. It ended up seeming so fruitless. I was never going to change my point of view and the religious person was never going to change theirs. I was sick of the endless treadmill. Although I do admit, they could still fire me up at that point in my life.

Occasionally, when I was approached by someone espousing religion, I would try to end it quickly with, "Sorry, I'm an atheist. I'm not interested."

They would give me a look as if I'd just confessed to being an axe murderer and then ask me how I could live a moral life without religion? It was hard for me to answer that question. On the one hand, I had my terrible secret of accidentally killing an innocent person and not confessing, which made me an extremely immoral person. However, on the other hand, in every other aspect of my life I'd tried to be as good and moral as I could be.

I wasn't promiscuous even when I was single. I didn't have sex until I was twenty. I was a person who drank virtually no alcohol until twenty-three and was faithful to my wife during our entire marriage. I'd never yelled at her or called her or the children a bad name. I'd tried to show respect towards everyone, avoided lying as much as possible and was kind to animals. I was brought up to be respectful just like most people and religion wasn't necessary to achieve that.

I found the most distressing part of religion for me was how various individuals or groups would be ostracised, whether it was atheists, Israelites, homosexuals, other religious groups or even people within that particular religion. Nyame wanted people to be accepted for who they were, with love and tolerance shown to everyone. Now I understand more of what the Afterlife is about and what it espouses but I can't help asking the questions I'm still not sure about.

Why do they denounce other religious groups? Why are they so intolerant of any opposing views? In the early days, many gay men were attracted to church life so they could hide behind the veil of celibacy and not have to explain why they didn't have a girlfriend or a wife. The churches were often aware of their priests' homosexuality, yet would still allow them to preach while condemning homosexuals. Similarly, there were paedophiles in the Church who were able to use their privileged positions of power and trust to abuse young children and remain uncensored.

Horrifically, many of these paedophiles were protected by the hierarchy of the Church. These were people who had spent their life in the pursuit of God, yet they seemed to be just as ignorant of their essence as I was.

Then there were the Evangelistic style leaders who would promise salvation if you would only give a bit more in the way of tithes. These people often became multi-millionaires and lived lavish lifestyles off the tithing of their flock. Money many of their congregation could ill afford. How did they expect salvation when they were doing the exact opposite of what they were asking their congregation to do? Is the problem with some of these leaders, that 'power corrupts and absolute power corrupts absolutely?'

Having said all that, on the opposite side of the spectrum, I have met some of the best people on the planet who have a strong religious faith. Their values, community spirit and compassion for others are second to none. It appears that a majority of religious people are in touch with their essence but perhaps are being blinded by the very organisation which is supposed to be helping them. Perhaps that was what Jesus was trying to say whilst standing on the temple steps imploring people not to go in?

When I'd compare the average Christian to the average atheist, I'd conclude the only meaningful difference between them was that one had decided the Bible was right and the other had decided that Science was right. Good people with different views. There were, however, other subtle differences. Many Christians believe that animals have been placed on the Earth to serve mankind, whereas some atheists, who believe in evolution, feel a very strong and special bond with the animal kingdom. When they look into the eyes of a chimpanzee they see an animal they believe is related to them.

DNA tells us we are more closely related to a chimpanzee than a gorilla is to a chimpanzee. Even a species of bird that is identical apart from their eye colour are more distantly related genetically, than humans to chimpanzees. Compare a red eyed Vireo bird to a white eyed Vireo and you get a greater genetic difference than a human to a chimp. With that evidence, evolutionists are understandably proud of the relationship they have with the ape family.

Consequently, there are a number of atheists who become vegetarians for humanitarian reasons, as I did myself in the latter stages of my life. I would rather eat a plant than have an animal suffer just to feed me. When I was on the Earth, the planet was having all sorts of environmental issues with global warming, destruction of the ozone layer, air, land and water pollution plus over population. Curiously, many Christians weren't that concerned. They were waiting for the second coming which apparently was just around the corner.

A number of the books I read on evolution were urging people to stop reproducing so quickly and to look at their food-producing methods such as reducing cattle numbers to combat the methane gas production which was causing so many environmental problems. The messages were loud and clear. All should take responsibility for a cleaner planet.

"At least, according to Niara, future generations appear to have got it right," I thought. "I have to be thankful for that."

Suddenly Niara appeared, nudging me from my reflections.

"Do you know the reason I am before you Grant?"

"Well no, not really. Is it because you missed all my questions and queries and decided to come back for more," I finished lamely.

Knowing Niara was with me for a reason sparked curiosity which was difficult to contain.

"Why ARE you here?"

"I need to ask you a question Grant. Do you feel prepared for your transition to the next stage? You may decline if you do not believe you are ready."

I felt a thrill of excitement and apprehension, the two emotions at war with each other. Quickly, excitement overpowered apprehension and the battle was won.

"Niara, I'm feeling fantastic and well prepared for wherever this transitional journey is going to take me."

"Do you have any idea what the next stage is going to be?" she asked cheekily.

"Not really, though I'm guessing it's too early for me to be a Guide, perhaps an observer on Earth? Come on Niara, give me a hint. I don't have a clue."

"Grant, you are to be re-birthed!" she exclaimed enthusiastically.

Stunned, I managed, "You mean I am going to be born back on Earth?"

"No Grant. You are going to be born into a very advanced alien civilisation in an entirely different galaxy and guess how long you can expect to live there?'

"I'm not good at guessing but I'd imagine it's longer than on Earth? Would it be three hundred to five hundred years maybe?" I hazarded.

"Try four times five hundred years!" Niara declared triumphantly.

"Are you saying that I'm going to live the life of an alien for two thousand years! Are you kidding me?" I managed to choke out.

"No Grant, I do not kid. Remember you are supposed to be the comedian of the two of us," and we both burst out laughing.

"Your new life will be very different this time. Firstly, you will inhabit a planet in a binary solar system," Niara disclosed.

"You mean there will be two suns?"

"Yes Grant. The planet is roughly four times larger than Earth with two suns and three moons. You will be quite dissimilar from that of a human. Are you excited about becoming an alien?"

"I have to say I'm not quite sure. I'd always believed in the likelihood of life on other planets but usually scoffed at people who'd reported they'd seen a UFO or had been abducted by aliens. It seemed to me very unlikely that an intelligent life form would be able to cover the vast distances of space required to make it to Earth and not leave a shred of real evidence upon arrival. Now I need to have a complete re-think and come to grips with the fact that I'm now going to be one of them," I explained, trying to mull over these new ideas before coming up with the obvious question.

"Has anyone from my new planet ever visited Earth?"

"Yes Grant but only twice has a visitor directly intervened with humankind. We do not encourage them to visit Earth. It may cause confusion for humans if they know too much."

"When did these visits occur?"

"Let me think. The first visit would have been over three thousand years before you died. He stayed for quite some time. There are stories of his visit recorded in a book on Earth."

"Really? I can't ever recall reading about something as important as that? What book was it in?"

"The book was called 'The Old Testament,' she replied blithely.

"What! I'm sorry Niara, but this time you're mistaken," I exclaimed. "I've read the Old Testament. There is definitely no mention of any alien visiting Earth."

"Ah Grant, sometimes you have to understand that what you think you are reading is not always what you are reading."

"Niara, you can think me obtuse but I'm not quite following you."

"Do you recall a story where Moses and the Israelites followed a silver cloud through the wilderness for forty years believing the cloud to be God?"

"Yes," I replied, wondering how this had anything to do with aliens on Earth.

"It was not God, Grant. It was one renegade from your re-birthing planet," was her astounding answer.

"No way! That's just too incredible. Are you positively sure?"

"Think carefully Grant. How would an ancient race describe something like a spaceship? Something they have absolutely no concept of?"

Now my thoughts were racing. How would they describe a spaceship? I surmised that a spaceship would likely be silvery in colour and to them it would appear most obviously....as a silver cloud! A silver cloud which stayed with them for forty years! I struggled to remember more of the story. It had been a long time since I'd last read that particular tale. How did it go again?

Fragments wafted in my mind waiting to be pulled together into something coherent. They gradually drifted together and my memory was restored.

"Niara, I recall that Moses parted the Red Sea after freeing the Israelites and fleeing from the Egyptians. Did the parting of the Red Sea actually occur?"

"In a way it did Grant. There was a hidden pathway across the Red Sea which had been built in anticipation of the exodus," Niara responded.

"Really! How was it hidden?"

"It was under the sea and could be raised or lowered."

"That's very clever. I still can't get over the fact the exodus story was actually true. Now let me think what else happened in that story."

Like a pot coming to the boil, more information bubbled to the forefront of my mind. I recalled that Moses and the Israelites were receiving information from the silver cloud and the unusual description of the cloud descending on Mount Sinai. The mountain was enveloped in a cloud and there was thunder and lightning and the voice of the trumpet exceedingly loud. The voice of God had warned the people not to get too close, especially when the cloud was descending, or they would die.

'The Lord descended upon it in fire and the mountain was covered in smoke and the whole mount quaked. The trumpet sounded long and waxed louder and louder.' Could that passage in the Bible possibly be describing a spaceship descending, retrorockets on fire, smoke and soil being blown into the air as a thick cloud? When I thought about it, even the sounds of a rocket in reverse thrust would be very loud and frightening and could be described as a trumpeting sound to people who didn't know better and it would have definitely shaken the ground beneath them.

Suddenly I remembered something else. Moses' face was shining so much after a long meeting with God atop the mountain that, "it frightened his followers so greatly that he was forced to wear a veil." Perhaps that was some sort of radiation burn? Maybe Moses got too close.

Another strange example was when they built a tabernacle. It was recorded the cloud would cover the tabernacle and no-one could enter until the cloud had ascended. During the day it was a cloud but at night it was fire.

"I wonder if that could have been the lights of the ship visible in the evening sky?"

This was all starting to make sense. It would explain the passage where Moses was forbidden to look upon the face of God. If, as Niara had said, the aliens looked different from us, it was highly probable that Moses and his followers would have had the heck scared out of them at any viewing.

"But then, what about the silver cloud leading the people into the Promised Land and actually helping them destroy some of the cities and people? Why would the alien have done that?" I posed to Niara. "What was his purpose for coming to Earth?"

"Kra was misguided Grant. He believed he was being helpful. He was trying to pass on information about Nyame and show a good way of living. Sadly, much of what he was trying to explain was misconstrued. For instance, he would never have advocated slavery as acceptable and he certainly would never have killed anyone."

"But the Bible had God slaughtering people by the thousands for working on the Sabbath and telling Moses' followers to kill every man, woman and child on entry into the Promised Land. God even helped them tear down cities. All that was associated with the same silver cloud," I spluttered indignantly.

"It did not happen Grant. Many of the stories have been altered to suit their culture at the time. The Bible described the people as being stiff necked and they were. They were very resistant to change and consequently re-wrote much of the information they received into their own version of history. Even archaeologists of your era supported the facts. They had never found one city which was destroyed in those particular areas mentioned or around that specific time period. There was no evidence to suggest a massive influx of people either, due to invasion or any other reason. It is all fabrication," Niara asserted.

After hearing this I couldn't get over how obvious it was and should have been to me all those years ago when I had been so diligently searching for ammunition against the Bible. It was apparent I hadn't seen the forest for the trees.

"When was the second visit?" I queried Niara.

"The second occurrence was a thousand years later Grant, but the coming was more discreet. After the abysmal failure with the Israelites, Kra almost gave up, but then decided to try once more with a single child, a Somalian girl by the name of Bad-weyn which means 'ocean'. It was an unusual choice of name for a child, but this child was very deep and the name was apt.

"Kra began to show her the places of the transitions so he could teach her to pass his messages on to the world as she grew. He wanted to educate her in cosmic hope and the meaning of life. From a very young age, Bad-weyn began to re-create the things which Kra showed her, through exquisite drawings. Her family was very poor but the child drew her pictures in the dust or used mud to express her art on the walls of her home.

"Everyone who saw her works delighted in them and knew she possessed the abilities of a genius. Not only did she possess a talent for drawing, she also devised poems to explain the teachings of Kra and the transitions. Do you wish to hear two of them Grant?"

"Yes please," I breathed, transfixed with this intriguing tale.

Niara paused and then her beautiful voice tinkled through my mind.

'The path from life
through death
Is hope

There guards from strife
with love
And joy

Contentment fills
beauty shines
in rainbow colours
Of the mind

My eyes are opened
the heart is swelled
Nothing is lost
all is well

Forever more
eternally
lessons will be learnt
Gratefully'

"Bad-weyn recited that poem to her mother when she was only three years
of age. The next poem was written shortly before her death and was titled
'Dashed the Tempest Coming'."

'The wondrous expression
From pictures show the way
An afterlife in heaven
Far beyond my starry gaze

From far flung galaxies
My mentor shows me how
Eternal life forsaken
If evil be thy sway

The road to salvation
Lies within and oft untapped
Nature brings thee closer
For mysteries unwrapped

Dashed the tempest coming
Do not waste thy years away
For the angels arrival
To taste your bitter wine

All good work will help you
In lessening the time
The black void awaiting
Abolishing misdeeds and crimes

Your pious walk in ignorance
Will keep you from rebirth
Listen closely to thy soul
While angels guide your way

A trillion souls required
In the next life and beyond
Each careful step along the way
Brings thee closer to redemption

The long and weary road
Will still be shared with many
So do not waste thy years away
Dashed the tempest coming.'

"I don't believe I could have explained it better even as an adult," I told Niara, deeply moved by the poignant poems. "What happened to Bad-weyn? I don't recall any dramatic impact on Earth's population because of this young girl's paintings and poetry?"

"No Grant. The experiment failed. Life was taken from Bad-weyn when she was seven years of age due to an unrelenting drought which decimated the country. Only her relatives and the people in her community were privy to her talent. Poverty contained her abilities so the world did not come to see her message," Niara concluded wistfully.

"In frustration, Kra returned home. He lived a long life. Perhaps you will get to meet him in the Afterlife one day?" Niara conjectured.

"But didn't he get punished, taken off the planet and sent back to therapy? If he was a renegade who acted outside the accepted way of doing things, surely he should have been corrected in some way?"

"Grant, no-one is perfect on the planet you are going to, just as no-one was perfect on Earth. There will be many learning experiences and challenges. Anything that cannot be handled will be repaired in two thousand years. Kra was well-meaning but deluded in his hopes of assisting mankind to achieve cosmic hope faster. He has learnt the errors of his ways," Niara declared.

"Grant, I must leave for final preparation. Think carefully of what I have told you and if you have any further questions, I will answer them on my return."

With that she was gone.

As usual, Niara left me with my head spinning. There have been so many twists and turns in this Afterlife journey so far and yet it seems to have just begun. Niara's story of Bad-weyn had reminded me of another prodigal child when I was alive on Earth. Her name was Akiane which was, stunningly, a Russian word for 'ocean.' Akiane was one of four children born to parents without a religious affiliation and was home schooled.

When Akiane was four years of age, her mother asked how she was one morning and the little girl said, "Today I met God. God is light, warm and good. It knows everything and talks with me. It is my parent. Where God takes me, he teaches me how to draw," she confided in her mother.

Of course, her mother did not believe her.

However, Akiane began to produce incredible pieces of artwork which were far beyond the capabilities of someone her age. Her parents were puzzled by her unusual talent and some of her distinctly different behaviours. For instance, the child could not stand any form of music whatsoever. Her mother was eventually reduced to tears at this, thinking that Akiane's dislike of music was an unreasonable response.

Akiane was five years old at the time and lifted her mother's tear-stained face in her hands.

"Mommy, please, please don't cry. I'm sorry I act this way but the music I hear in Heaven is better than here. This music hurts my ears and my head really bad, but heavenly music is always gentle. I can't tell you how different it is from what you hear on Earth. It feels like joy, looks like love, smells like flowers and dances like butterflies. Music there is alive! You can even taste it," she explained to her parent.

At seven years of age she began to compose profound poetry almost effortlessly. Her paintings took hours or hundreds of hours to complete whilst she could often compose a poem within half an hour. By the time

Akiane was ten; her paintings were selling for $10,000. Two years later, they were fetching $250,000 each.

One of her paintings titled 'Returning Home' was described by Akiane in this way: "Entrance into the unknown is the entrance into eternal life full of different dimensions, energies, times, personalities, spirits and choices, where the levels of experiences are beyond our imagination. Here planets symbolizing souls return back to their designer for new assignments, new adventures, new relationships and new challenges." Akiane was only twelve years old when she wrote that. By the time I died, Akiane was in her teens and still painting and writing prolifically.

The similarities between her and Bad-weyn are uncanny. How could she have heard the music? Could Akiane have tapped into someone like Kra, or maybe she had accessed her essence at a much greater level? I hope I get to meet her in this next life. She will know by then what it was all about.

I felt likewise with Kra. He sounds as if his heart was in the right place even if things didn't work out as he'd wanted them to. Kra appears as if he'd be a pretty interesting character and I'd love to hear his version of events with the Israelites. I couldn't help but marvel at the thought of meeting him, although realising I wouldn't get the opportunity till I'd finished with this next life.

Niara suddenly materialised, watching and waiting for the next inevitable question.

"Niara, everything I have learnt here has been fascinating and educational, but will I remember any of this after I'm re-birthed?"

"You will be born with all your conscious and subconscious memories, so you will be able to have many more of your questions answered," Niara promised.

"That will be fantastic, almost unbelievable. To be born with all that information; what a head start I'll have."

"Everyone is in the same position Grant. Every single member of your new race has been re-birthed from human kind. Every acceptable human for the last one hundred thousand years has gone through this process. This is a very advanced civilization. What you will experience there will alter your perceptions forever. The good news is you will have a far greater capacity to learn than in human form."

"Niara, what truly is the purpose of all this learning? Is it absolutely necessary?"

Not that I was complaining, although I will admit to times of being overwhelmed by the astonishing amounts of information which attacked my foundations to the core.

"Yes Grant," Niara responded steadfastly. "There are things you are going to experience which will prove to be very beneficial in your long journey ahead. Remember, you are going to be around for eternity. There are many phases before your final transition and you will require much learning. And Grant, one more thing; there are no atheists on this planet. They are all Believers, just as you are now," she advised with a mischievous twinkle in her voice.

"What an odyssey," I thought.

"Sixty years on Earth which went so fast it was like a dream. Well over two hundred years in the transitions and yet that time appeared to go even faster. Now I'm journeying into an unknown realm where I might end up living for two thousand years before I end up who knows where? I bet no-one on Earth could have ever predicted anything like this!"

"It is almost time Grant," Niara prompted me.

"Niara, you said I would retain my memories. Will I meet my friends and family from Earth on this planet?"

"If you or they choose to you will," was her odd reply. "Please recall that every person's journey is different. Some of your friends and family may already be on the planet, even if they died after you. Some may be thousands of years away from being re-birthed," she deliberated. "The relationships you had on Earth may be vastly contrasting to the relationships you could form on your new planet," Niara warned. "Grant, you are very close to entering the portal and being re-born. Do you have any final questions?"

"Just one Niara. What is the final transition? What is our ultimate purpose?"

"Grant, I am sorry but you are not ready for the answers to those questions yet," she admonished me gently. "All I can say is that Nyame's ultimate purpose for all of us is so incredible, so unbelievable, that you would not be able to guess what the answer was, even if you puzzled about it for the rest of eternity. Happily, you will not have to wait that long; you will be ready for the answers on your return. Have a great life Grant and if Nyame is willing, I will see you in two thousand years. Oh, and by the way, that was two questions, not one," I heard her laughing gaily.

Then she was gone before I'd had a chance to say a proper goodbye. Almost instantly I was caught up in a vortex of immense power. I could feel blackness, being forced down and a tightening band across my chest. Struggling for breath in this confined space, I tried to force my way out… Suddenly I could breathe and then a blinding light. Oh my God! I didn't expect this...

THE END

AUSTRALIAN EXPRESSIONS

arvo – afternoon

arse – backside

Aussie – person from Australia

barbie – barbecue or BBQ

barra – a barramundi fish

battler – struggling working class person

Beyond the Black Stump – far from the city; the outback

Bikie – motorcyclist

Billabong – waterhole

bingle – minor car accident

blighter – devious person

bloke – man

bludge – avoid work / try to get something for free

bludger – layabout, one who wants something for nothing, person who does not work or works very little

bogan – vulgar and uncouth person

booze – alcohol

booze up – alcoholic drinking session

brickie – bricklayer / mason

buckleys – no chance

bugging – annoying

bugger – damn / mischievous person

bum – backside / no-hoper

bushfire – wildfire

bushie – someone from rural area

burl – 'give it a burl' give it a go; attempt something

by crickey – an expression of surprise

cactus – useless, broken

calling it quits – stopping / giving up

cark it – to die

carton – 24 cans or bottles of beer

cashed up – having plenty of ready money

cheesed (off) – bored; fed up

chemist – drug store / pharmacy

cheers – thanks / salutations

chippie – carpenter

chook – domestic fowl

chuck a wobbly – go berserk

cobber – friend

cocky – know all; also a farmer

come a cropper – to fall heavily

 dead set – certain; assured; used as an exclamation meaning 'really!'

dead set against it – uncooperative

digger – soldier

dinky-di – genuine

dob in – to betray or report someone to the authorities

doing the hard yards – working hard

drongo – stupid person

dunny – an outside toilet

esky – a portable icebox (brand name)

fair dinkum – honest; genuine

fair enough – alright; acceptable

fair go – a chance; also an appeal for fairness

faze – to disturb / to daunt

fossick – to search for something

freak out – to have an extreme reaction (good or bad) to something

garbage – an exclamation meaning 'what rubbish, I don't believe you!'

garbo – garbage collector

git – stupid person

go for your life – to try as hard as you can

good one – an explanation of approval; or comment that someone is stretching the truth

goon – hired thug / wine

greeny – environmentalist

gutful – more than enough (I've had a gutful of this – I've had enough)

have tickets on yourself – to be conceited

head starting to spin – feeling of confusion

heaps – many / a lot of teasing

hit the deck – to duck; to put your head down

hoon – a stupid or uncultivated person; also a fast or reckless driver

hooroo – goodbye

kid – child

kiwi – New Zealander

knock – to criticise, find fault

knocker – a person who criticises

larrikin – mischievous, wild or carefree person

lingo – language

maccas – McDonalds

magpie – Australian native bird

main drag – main road or street through a town

mate – good or best friend; also used to greet someone as in 'G'day mate'

muff – to bungle

mug – fool

mulga – rough country (actually: a type of tree)

muso – musician

no-hoper – incompetent person; social misfit

no worries – no problems / everything is alright

nick – to steal

nick off – to go away; expression meaning 'lose yourself!'

ocker – the archetypal uncultivated Australian male

oi – way to get attention

outback – the inland country far away from large cities

out of her hair – out of her way

pint of beer – 570ml

pom / pommy – English person

panadols – headache tablets

prang – minor car accident

prank – a mischievous trick

prawn – shrimp

petrol – gasoline

pot of beer – 285ml Also known as a 'middy' or 'handle'

rack off – to go away

ratbag – a rogue; an eccentric person

reckon – to think or suppose

rego – vehicle registration

righto – alright

ring-in – a substitute

road train – a truck with multiple trailers attached

rort – a con

rubbish – to criticise; to mock

schooner of beer – 425ml

servo – a petrol station or gas station

shoot through – to go somewhere else (or he shot through)

shonky – poor quality

shotgun – the front passenger seat of a vehicle

shout – to buy drinks for everyone

sickie – a day taken off work, but not necessarily because of illness

skite – a bragger

slack – lazy

smoko – a break from work (originally a cigarette)

sparkie – electrician

speedo – vehicle speedometer

stubby – a bottle of beer (375ml) or stubbie / a brand of shorts

stubby cooler – container used to keep a stubby or can of beer cold

swag – a blanket roll of light bedding

take-away – fast food place / food 'to go'

the bush – uncultivated rural areas

tinnie – a can of beer; a small aluminium boat

to have the wind [as in breeze] up you – to frighten you

too right – an exclamation meaning 'I agree'

top drop – a good beer or wine

true blue – genuine

tucker – food

twit – a fool

undies – underwear

ute – open backed pick-up truck

veg out – relax

wag – to play truant

wanker – annoying or dislikeable person

watch your back – support and protect you

wheelie – a noisy skidding turn while driving

whinge – to complain

whopper – something surprisingly big

woop- woop – out in the middle of no where

wowser – a killjoy; a prudish teetotaller

write-off – a total loss

wuss – spoilsport; afraid to have a go

yakka – hard or heavy work

yank – American

yeah, yep – yes

yobbo – a loud or stupid uncultivated person